"I want you to work for me, exclusively," he said.

"But that's absurd!" Casey exclaimed. "I run a *business*, Mr. Stoner. I'd be willing to let you hire one of my chefs, but I'm not for sale."

"Uh uh," he growled. "I want you."

Casey was vibrantly aware of her body and its reactions to Matt's presence just a few feet away. His low, insistent voice throbbed with a sensual quality. "Come to the Cape with me, Casey."

Then he was beside her on the couch, and there was no more need for pretense. She felt his fingers fasten firmly on her chin and turn her face to his. Her lips parted to protest, but how could she say anything when his lips were covering hers and his tongue was beginning a slow, voluptuous exploration of her mouth? His tongue was like fire, probing and circling and making love to her, unhurriedly, deliberately seducing her into abandon.

"Come to the Cape with me," he whispered.

Dear Reader:

As the months go by, we continue to receive word from you that SECOND CHANCE AT LOVE romances are providing you with the kind of romantic entertainment you're looking for. In your letters you've voiced enthusiastic support for SECOND CHANCE AT LOVE, you've shared your thoughts on how personally meaningful the books are, and you've suggested ideas and changes for future books. Although we can't always reply to your letters as quickly as we'd like, please be assured that we appreciate your comments. Your thoughts are all-important to us!

We're glad many of you have come to associate SECOND CHANCE AT LOVE books with our butterfly trademark. We think the butterfly is a perfect symbol of the reaffirmation of life and thrilling new love that SECOND CHANCE AT LOVE heroines and heroes find together in each story. We hope you keep asking for the "butterfly books," and that, when you buy one—whether by a favorite author or a talented new writer—you're sure of a good read. You can trust all SECOND CHANCE AT LOVE books to live up to the high standards of romantic fiction you've come to expect.

So happy reading, and keep your letters coming!

With warm wishes,

Ellen Edwards

Ellen Edwards
SECOND CHANCE AT LOVE
The Berkley/Jove Publishing Group
200 Madison Avenue
New York, NY 10016

A MAN'S PERSUASION
KATHERINE GRANGER

SECOND CHANCE AT LOVE
BOOK

For E—

1

CASEY ADAMS PUT the final touches on the elaborate menu she was planning, then sat back to inspect it. Pushing her horn-rimmed glasses onto her glossy chestnut-colored hair, she ran her green eyes over the menu of classic French cooking, elegantly scripted on thick ivory parchment. Nibbling on the tip of the pen, Casey debated about the first course. Should she serve the *foie gras* as she had originally planned or would a galantine of duck be better?

Leaning back, she thought about the huge formal dining room at the Bentley mansion in Louisburg Square. With its hand-painted French wallpaper, sparkling crystal chandeliers, and shining mahogany table, the room would be a magnificent setting for either the *foie gras* or the duck.

"Enough of this indecision," she said out loud, putting the menu to one side. "We'll go with the *foie gras.*"

Now the hard part would begin—ordering the meat, vegetables, and fish; selecting the wines; choosing the china and table linens; charting all the intricate details involved in orchestrating a sit-down dinner for eighteen people.

Not that Casey minded. Since starting her catering and cleaning business, Maid To Order, five years ago, she could honestly say she had never minded a single day's work. And now, after years of hard, unrelenting labor, she was able to take it a little easier. Money was pouring in, with no hint of ever stopping. A local paper had done an article this past weekend on the ten most successful businesswomen in Boston and she had headed the list. She had come a long way from the frightened, wide-eyed twenty-two-year-old who had scrubbed bathroom tiles in Beacon Hill town-houses.

A soft buzz interrupted Casey's thoughts. She lifted the receiver and punched the blinking button on the phone.

"Casey Adams."

"Pamela Tyrone, Mrs. Adams, from Stoner Enterprises."

At the mention of Stoner Enterprises, Casey sat up, slipping her glasses off her head and putting them firmly in place on her nose. The voice that wafted across the phone lines was low and throaty, tinged with just the right amount of refinement and breeding.

"Yes, Miss Tyrone," Casey answered. "How may I help you?"

"I'm calling for Mr. Stoner. He asked me to set up a meeting with you. We'd like to discuss the possibility of your doing some work for him. Would you be free tomorrow?"

"Mr. Stoner?" Casey asked, trying to sound vague. It wouldn't do to let on that she had immediately recognized the name of the most talked-about business tycoon in Boston. His name was in every society sheet, in every gossip column, on the tip of every hostess's tongue. Handsome, virile, and rich, he was the epitome of Boston society.

"Mr. Matthew Stoner," Pamela Tyrone said, emphasiz-

ing his name in a way that indicated everyone should know
who *he* was.

"Oh, yes," Casey murmured, a hint of a smile playing
at her lips. *"That* Mr. Stoner. Did you say tomorrow?" She
ran her eyes over her packed calendar. "I'm afraid I couldn't
meet with him tomorrow. Would Thursday be all right?"

A throaty laugh came over the phone lines. "Oh, you
won't be meeting with Mr. Stoner, Mrs. Adams. He's much
too busy to speak with you in person. *I'll* be speaking with
you in his place."

"I see. . . ." Casey lifted an eyebrow. Just who *was* this
Pamela Tyrone? For some reason, this woman was subtly
making Casey feel as if she were one of the domestic maids
she employed, rather than the owner and manager of a highly
successful business. Not that there was anything wrong with
being a maid. Casey herself had started out that way and
she had the highest regard for the hard-working women who
formed the backbone of her organization. Five years ago,
when she was just starting her company, this kind of snob-
bish tone of voice had bothered her, but long years of dealing
with the super-rich had given Casey poise and the ability
to laugh off the disparaging remarks of haughty clients. But
those remarks had died out years ago, when it became ap-
parent that Casey was not only extraordinarily good at what
she did, but also every inch a lady. As the recent article in
the paper had said, it was often difficult to tell Casey apart
from her distinguished clients. With her stunning good looks
and expensively tailored clothes, she was as much at home
in the elegant drawing rooms as in the kitchen concocting
elaborate dishes.

But this hadn't been simply the snide comment of a
thoughtless dowager. There had been a special barb in Pamela Tyrone's cool voice. A slight frown wrinkled her forehead, but Casey shrugged away her doubts.

"I'm very sorry, Miss Tyrone," she said cordially, "but
I just can't see my way clear to meet with you tomorrow.
I'm absolutely jammed with appointments. Perhaps I could
send my assistant, Miss Simpson?"

"I'm so sorry, Mrs. Adams," Pamela Tyrone purred,

"but Mr. Stoner asked expressly for you. He said no one else would do."

The frown on Casey's face deepened. There it was again, a smug tone in that smooth voice that subtly conveyed disdain, as if Miss Tyrone thought she were speaking to an underling. But why? As far as she knew, Casey had never even met Miss Tyrone. What could be Pamela Tyrone's reason for disliking her? Was Miss Tyrone somehow echoing her boss's feelings? Was it Matthew Stoner who thought Casey wasn't important enough to meet with him?

Arching a brow, Casey scratched the tip of her pen across a pad of paper, leaving deeply etched, black strokes. This called for decisive action. If Matthew Stoner wanted her to work for him, he would have to meet with her in person, no middlemen.

"I quite understand Mr. Stoner's position, Miss Tyrone," Casey said. "In fact, I feel exactly the same way. No one but Mr. Stoner will do for me, either. Perhaps you'd explain to him that I'm completely booked tomorrow and arrange for a meeting on Thursday. I'd be happy to meet with him at his convenience."

Casey got the feeling that Pamela Tyrone was looking daggers at the phone, but she recovered gamely. That low laugh drifted through the receiver, tinged with rueful disdain. "I'll speak with him, Mrs. Adams. There's always the possibility that he could squeeze you in late in the day. Would that be suitable?"

"Perfectly suitable, Miss Tyrone," Casey said, scribbling a note to keep Thursday afternoon open. After a murmured good-bye, the phone went dead and Casey dropped the receiver back in its cradle with a bemused laugh.

Casey's assistant stuck her head around the door and joined her laughter. "While we're laughing, mind telling me what it's all about?" Joanie Simpson asked.

Casey's face held a puzzled look. "I've just had the strangest phone call, Joanie," she said, motioning her to sit down. Then she laughed softly and shrugged, deciding she was imagining Pamela Tyrone's dislike of her. "Actually,

I think I've finally made it. Know who that call was from?"

Joanie screwed up her pretty face and bit at her lip. "The mayor?" she asked, then shook her head quickly. "No, we've done plenty of work for him." She raised one eyebrow comically and cocked her head to one side. "The president?"

Casey laughed and shook her head, then leaned forward to put special emphasis on her words. "Pamela Tyrone."

"Pamela Tyrone," Joanie repeated blankly. "Okay, I give up—who's Pamela Tyrone?"

Casey's look was rueful. "From the sound of her, she's the most important person in Boston. Know what makes her so important?"

Joanie shook her head.

"She works for Matthew Stoner."

Joanie's face changed dramatically, registering stunned comprehension. "Matthew Stoner!" she whispered reverently. "My God, Casey, you *have* arrived!"

Casey sat back and crossed her shapely legs. "Well, maybe I have and maybe I haven't. In fact, I might have just blown it."

"How? And if you did, why in tarnation are you laughing about it? I'd say you should be pulling out the crying towel."

"Maybe I'm just getting too independent for my own good, Joanie, but it rubbed me the wrong way when Miss Tyrone implied that I wasn't important enough to meet with Matthew Stoner in person." She shrugged nonchalantly, her green eyes sparkling mischievously. "So I just put my foot down—very nicely, of course—and insisted that Stoner meet with me in person if he wants me to work for him." Laughter bubbled to the surface once again. "I got the distinct impression that Pamela Tyrone thought I was being awfully presumptuous."

"So you think you've cooked your own goose?"

"If I haven't, then Pamela Tyrone just might. And from the sound of her, she might do more than just cook it—she might just sneak into the kitchen and poison it!"

"Well . . ." Joanie shrugged. "Who needs Matthew Stoner anyway?" she asked bravely, then her head sank into her hands. "But, Casey, how *could* you? You *know* you've always wanted to work for him! And how else am I ever going to get to see him in person?"

"Take heart, Joanie," Casey grinned. "If Matthew Stoner thinks I'm good enough, he'll talk with me in person. If he doesn't, then who needs him?"

"Well, if you look at it like that...."

"What other way is there to look at it? But let's not start worrying now. Let's wait until we hear an explosion coming from the direction of the Stoner Building."

Joanie grinned and stood up to leave. "You're right, Casey—but do you have to prove it on Matthew Stoner?"

Casey laughed, her thoughts already returning to business. "Here's the menu for the Bentley dinner party," she said, holding out the parchment page to Joanie. "Set up a time for me to go over and choose the china and linen, will you? And call the florist and ask him to make sure he's got scads of orchids. And, oh, Joanie—" Casey's eyes registered the note she had scribbled on her calendar. "Hold Thursday afternoon open for me, please. If the great Mr. Stoner will deign to meet with me, that's when it will be."

"Will do," Joanie said, jotting down notes as she walked out of the office.

Casey watched Joanie leave, then slipped off her glasses and twirled them in one hand, her eyes surveying the comfortable blend of antiques, cushioned couches and chairs that furnished her office. The walls were a pristine white, and the tall windows were uncurtained. A warm, chocolate-brown carpet covered the floor, and the furniture was upholstered in oatmeal cotton. Blue-and-white bargello pillows were scattered on the couches and chairs, echoing the blue and white of the oriental bowls that held fresh flowers on the shining pine tables.

Casey knew the office was a serene backdrop for her own dramatic coloring: chestnut hair and green eyes. She pictured how she must appear to her clients, dressed in her finest Irish wools and English tweeds. Her blouses were silk and her shoes of the finest Italian leather—the garb of a rich and successful businesswoman.

Casey sighed, put on her glasses, and made a teasing face to herself. In five years she had reached the point in her life where it seemed that the only challenge awaiting her was the possibility of a phone call from Pamela Tyrone telling her that Matthew Stoner would see her personally.

"Ah, sweet success," she murmured ironically. "To think that it all comes down to a phone call from a man."

Casey was elbow deep in papers the next day when the telephone rang. Reaching out, she pushed the blinking light and picked up the receiver, her thoughts still absorbed by the menu she was planning.

"Casey Adams."

"Pamela Tyrone, Mrs. Adams."

Casey's mind cleared immediately. "Yes, Miss Tyrone," she answered politely, feeling her heart give a little lurch of excitement. "How are you today?"

Pamela ignored the pleasantry and plunged straight into business. "Mr. Stoner will see you tomorrow afternoon at five P.M. sharp. You'll be free to see him, I presume?"

Casey frowned at the chilly tone, but suppressed a sigh and nodded. "Of course. Five o'clock. I'll be there. Where would Mr. Stoner like to meet me?"

"At his executive offices," Pamela Tyrone said coolly. "The penthouse. Stoner Enterprises Building."

"Stoner Building . . ." Casey murmured, writing the words on her calendar. "Let's see, I believe I know where that is. . . ."

"Everyone knows the Stoner Building, Mrs. Adams," Pamela said haughtily. "It's the triangle-shaped building on the waterfront. The one that won the Architects Award of the Year last year, the one that Mr. Stoner designed himself. *Surely* you know it, Mrs. Adams."

Casey felt grim laughter threatening to escape. "Oh, yes, I seem to remember now—the one where the ragged old docks used to be."

There was a momentary silence, then a cool, haughty "yes," came over the phone, causing Casey to grin to herself. No, there was no use getting around it—for some reason,

Pamela Tyrone had taken a dislike to Casey, sight unseen. Shrugging mentally, Casey forced herself to murmur a polite good-bye, then hung up the phone.

As she turned back to her work, her eyes fell on the picture of herself that smiled up from the pages of Sunday's newspaper. The photograph had been taken when she was interviewed for the article. It was a particularly flattering likeness, shot while she was seated at her desk, her glasses held in one hand, a soft smile illuminating her features as she flipped through a cookbook.

Casey picked up the paper and stuffed it in the wastepaper basket. Joanie had left it out for her to save if she wanted it. Casey sighed. Her mother had died just after Casey had married Andy. Her father had been dead since she was a sophomore in high school. And Andy, of course, was gone, had been for five years. There was no one to save it for.

Bending her head, Casey plunged into her work again, all thoughts of Pamela Tyrone and Matthew Stoner lost amid the welter of cookbooks and papers that were scattered on her desk.

Casey angled her car into a parking place and peered up at the mirror façade of the Stoner Enterprises Building. Twenty-five stories up, in the penthouse, Matthew Stoner would be waiting for her. She ran a slim hand over the hair that framed her face in thick, curving waves and ended in a cascade of curls at her shoulders. With her glasses and gray tweed suit, she was the consummate businesswoman. Briefly she wondered what Matthew Stoner would think of her.

From all accounts he was very much the ladies' man. He had the reputation of loving and leaving them, often in the space of a single night. At thirty-six he was already a multimillionaire, but none of the Boston dowagers had succeeded in snaring him for their daughters.

A wry smile curved Casey's generous mouth. From the pictures of the women she had seen on his arm, Casey didn't think she would suit him. His taste seemed to run to tall, svelte black-haired model types, willowy blonds, and lush brunettes. There hadn't been a redhead among them—not that she was a redhead, Casey qualified. She had always been pleased that her gleaming mahogany hair was much too rich and dark to be called red, yet had too much of a chestnut sheen to be called brunette.

Casey's eyes glittered in amusement as she slid from the car. She thought it would be interesting to meet this paragon of masculinity, but doubted that he would appeal to her. In the past five years she hadn't met a man who could duplicate the soaring euphoria that her beloved Andy had engendered in her. Casey had resigned herself to dating a series of good-looking, well-to-do men who either left her totally unmoved when they kissed her or who chased her around her apartment at the end of the evening, all the while explaining that they knew widows needed consoling and they were more than willing to lend a hand.

Casey slammed the car door with remembered anger. Just two weeks ago she had gone out with a devastatingly attractive man, only to have him try to put his hand up her dress under the table at one of the best Boston restaurants. Furious, she had stood up, thrown her napkin onto the table, and strode out of the restaurant, leaving "one of the prime catches in Boston" open-mouthed in amazement.

Casey was beginning to wonder if there were any nice men left, men who took a woman out and didn't expect her to go to bed with them on the first date, or even on the second. Men like Andy. . . .

Casey suddenly realized she was standing at the imposing entrance to the Stoner Building, lost in thought, blocking the way for two impatient businessmen behind her. Flashing a smile that mollified them, she swung open the door and strode across the lobby, toward the elevators. Her eyes twinkled as she caught sight of the admiring glances cast her way by the two men who had followed her into the building.

"Sorry, fellas," she murmured under her breath as she entered the elevator and pushed P for penthouse. "I'm not interested."

In what seemed like seconds the elevator doors opened noiselessly, revealing a quiet corridor carpeted in thick gray wool. The walls were paneled in expensive rosewood. Two glass doors directly in front of the elevator announced in ornate gold lettering that these were the Executive Offices, Stoner Enterprises.

Casey pushed open the doors and found herself in a reception room. The same gray carpeting covered the floor. Black leather chairs and couches of sleek design sat beside glass-and-steel tables that held neat stacks of the latest business and finance magazines. Green plants flourished under modern track lighting. On the white walls there was a series of black-and-white abstract prints matted in red. At a mammoth glass-topped desk a young blond woman sat tapping her long pink nails on the desk's surface.

Casey decided this couldn't be Pamela Tyrone. The young woman's face was much too innocent and open. As if reading Casey's thoughts, the girl looked up and smiled warmly.

"You must be Mrs. Adams. Miss Tyrone is expecting you."

"Miss Tyrone?" Casey faltered slightly. "I believe my appointment is with Mr. Stoner." She wondered uneasily if Matthew Stoner had tricked her into coming to an appointment with his assistant instead of himself.

"Oh, yes, you'll be seeing Mr. Stoner," the receptionist assured her, "but Miss Tyrone always sees Mr. Stoner's visitors first."

"I see." Casey smiled in relief. She was tempted to ask if Miss Tyrone also checked for weapons while inspecting Mr. Stoner's visitors, but resisted the impulse, turning away instead to let her eyes sweep the reception area. A few seconds later she turned back to the receptionist, who was on the phone.

"Miss Tyrone?" the young girl was saying. "Mrs. Adams is here." The expression on the girl's face altered slightly, as if Pamela Tyrone were saying something that made her uneasy. She glanced up at Casey and looked away again quickly. "Yes, Miss Tyrone, I'll tell her." The girl hung up and hesitated, biting at her lip. When she looked up at Casey her eyes were worried. "Miss Tyrone says to tell you to go right in to see Mr. Stoner. He's . . . he's expecting you."

Satisfaction washed over Casey. She hadn't particularly wanted to see Pamela Tyrone and was just as happy to bypass her completely. The receptionist pointed Casey down a long, quiet hallway and then hesitated again. "Er . . . Miss Tyrone said to tell you not to knock. She said you could go right in." The girl looked away uneasily, still gnawing at her bottom lip.

Casey smiled, thanked her, then headed down the hall that led to Matthew Stoner's office. Whatever Pamela Tyrone had said to the receptionist had certainly upset her, but that hardly surprised Casey. Casey had the distinct impression that Pamela Tyrone treated most people as if they were floor mats. She had probably been as rude to the young girl as she had been to Casey on the phone.

As she approached the double doors at the end of the hall, Casey felt an unfamiliar surge of apprehension. Butterflies swirled in her stomach. She put her hand on the door knob as she reassured herself. She wasn't a naive twenty-two-year-old from South Boston any longer. She was a wealthy, successful businesswoman. Why should these plushly carpeted corridors unnerve her?

The answer floated up from her subconscious, surprising her with its intensity. "Because," a voice said, "deep down inside you really *are* still that frightened little girl from Southie. And when you rub up against *real* power and *real* money, you revert to type."

Casey angrily squared her shoulders. Nonsense! She was the new. Casey Adams, unafraid of anything, mistress of her own fate, a woman alone who had succeeded against all odds.

Raising her chin combatively, Casey turned the doorknob and stepped into Matthew Stoner's office, then stopped dead. Directly in front of her, locked in a passionate embrace, were a man and a woman, oblivious to her presence. The woman stood on tiptoe, her high heels discarded on the floor, one leg raised in a classic pose from the movies of the thirties and forties. She was bent back over the man's muscular arm, her golden hair flowing down to her waist, but not covering up the fact that the zipper of her dress was partially undone, allowing the man's hand easy access to her bare back and shoulders.

As Casey stood and watched, that hand moved sensuously over the woman's back and pushed at the fabric of the dress as if it were a mild annoyance. When he began to strip the dress from her shoulders, Casey realized she had to do something—or risk further and worse embarrassment.

But what could she do? She was standing by the open doors of the office, debating whether to clear her throat or try to slip away quietly, when Matthew Stoner raised his head and saw her.

2

IN THE SPACE of a second, Casey saw Matthew Stoner's eyes change from slumbering sensuality to fierce anger. What had been warm gray depths became flinty granite chips. In that same instant Casey registered everything about him, from the deep tan of his craggy face to the unruly black hair that tumbled over his forehead and grew in curling rebellion onto his strong neck. His white shirt was open at the collar and his tie was pulled down, revealing crisp black hair that welled up from his muscular chest. His shirtsleeves were rolled up to the elbows, displaying the sinewed forearms of a dock worker. In that split second he was the picture of an angry, wild pirate. Casey could imagine him dressed in tight pants with a flowing white shirt straining across his chest muscles and a sword in his hand, standing on the bow of his ship, ready to fight the entire world.

In the next second he was civilized again, taking hold of the woman and firmly turning her so that her back was to Casey.

"We appear to have a visitor, Crystal," he murmured smoothly. "Perhaps you'd better zip up, hmmm?"

The woman named Crystal screeched and awkwardly reached behind to zip up her dress, her face beet red as she slipped into her discarded shoes.

"Will I see you tonight, Matt?" she asked, casting an anxious glance at Matthew Stoner.

He was leaning nonchalantly against his desk, one muscular thigh draped along its edge, a long, slim cigar at his lips. He struck a match and held it to the cigar tip and puffed lazily, then shook out the match. His eyes were indulgent as he glanced at Crystal.

"Perhaps. We'll see. I'll call you if I'm coming. You'd better run along now."

Crystal nodded and hurried toward the door, which still stood open. Casey was shocked to see that Crystal couldn't have been more than nineteen or twenty. She flung a rebellious look at Casey, then flounced out of the office and slammed the door shut behind her.

Casey took a deep breath and slowly raised her eyes to Matthew Stoner. He was still lounging against his desk, and his eyes were roaming over her, taking in the simple but costly gold chain that circled her slim neck, the richness of her fine silk shirt, the expensive cut of her Irish tweed suit. His eyes lingered on her legs, then traveled slowly upward to her face.

"And who might you be?" he asked lazily.

Casey straightened, raising her chin a fraction of an inch. "I'm Casey Adams. We have a five o'clock appointment, I believe."

He raised an inquiring eyebrow. "Do we?" He glanced at his watch, amusement entering his gray eyes. "Judging by the way you show up precisely on the dot, it's a good thing we didn't have an appointment for five fifteen. . . ."

Casey's face flamed with color. "I was told to be here precisely at five, Mr. Stoner," she said coolly. "And I always try to please my customers."

"An interesting thought, Mrs. Adams," he replied, his eyes indolently assessing her figure once again. "And one I'll try to keep in mind in the future." At the angry look on Casey's face, one corner of his mouth lifted in wry amusement. He pushed away from his desk and gestured toward a chair near his desk. "Take a seat, Mrs. Adams, and explain yourself."

"Explain myself?" Puzzled, Casey looked up at him as she sank into the leather chair. "I don't understand."

He eased his tall frame into the chair behind his desk and fixed her with steel-gray eyes. "You don't really think you're going to get off that easily, do you?"

"Get *off?*" she repeated blankly. "What are you talking about?"

"I'm talking about the way you barged into my office just now without being announced," he explained in a tight voice. "Miss Tyrone, who guards my office like a tiger, would never have let that happen, so it had to be your doing. Do you care to explain why you feel you're entitled to circumvent my office procedures?"

Hot anger surged through Casey's Irish veins. Wasn't it just like a man to jump to conclusions? Anyone else would have politely ignored what had happened, but not Matthew Stoner! Frustrated, Casey could only sit and stare at him, not knowing how to tell him that Pamela Tyrone had ordered the receptionist to tell her to go straight into his office without even knocking.

But why? Pamela Tyrone must have known he had a visitor—and what a visitor! At the memory of what she had walked in on, Casey's face reddened again. She glanced at Matthew Stoner and saw that the steel had left his eyes. Now they held only quiet amusement—amusement at her expense. With the slim cigar held lightly between his strong white teeth, he looked like some medieval lord. One thumb rubbed his chin with mesmerizing, almost sensual slowness.

"Well, Mrs. Adams?" he prompted. "Nothing to say to defend yourself?"

How she would like to slap that maddening look off his arrogant face! Instead, she lowered her eyes and schooled herself to remain calm. What good would it to do try to explain? Obviously he had complete faith in Pamela Tyrone. Casey's criticizing her would only make Casey look bad. Better to leave it that there had been a mix-up—and that was probably the correct explanation anyhow.

Suppressing a sigh, Casey lifted her eyes to Matthew Stoner's. "There must have been a misunderstanding, Mr. Stoner," she said quietly. "I must have misunderstood what the receptionist said after she'd spoken with Miss Tyrone. I thought she said go right in without knocking first. She must have said the opposite." Her eyes flickered away from those knowing ones. "Believe me, I wouldn't have walked in on you if I'd known . . ." She faltered, feeling her face go red again. "I mean, if I'd expected . . . well . . ." She was fumbling and stumbling all over the place, and Matthew Stoner wasn't making it any easier on her.

She glanced up and saw him take the cigar from his mouth and lean forward to place it in an ashtray. Casey watched the muscles ripple in his shoulders and upper arms as the fabric of his shirt stretched against his body. She forced herself to look away quickly, but encountered his speculative eyes and felt another blush creeping up her neck into the creamy ivory of her face.

Silently she cursed a complexion that reflected her loss of composure so readily. What was it about this man that rattled her so? It must be just the situation, she told herself. Anyone, even the most experienced, worldly woman, would have been momentarily put off her balance by coming upon a man making love to such a willing partner. It was an embarrassing situation for everyone involved, and if Matthew Stoner looked cool and unruffled, it had more to do with his callousness than with Casey's lack of sophistication.

"We may as well forget the entire episode, Mrs. Adams. May I trust your discretion? I don't worry about my own

reputation—it went to the devil years ago—but I do want
to protect Crystal's. She's young and impulsive. I'd hate to
see her hurt."

Casey bit back a caustic remark, forcing her face to
remain impassive. Inwardly, though, she nodded knowingly.

Oh, sure, she thought bitterly. You're worried about
Crystal—over my dead body you are!

How she detested men like Matthew Stoner! They were
greedy and lusting, caring only about satisfying their own
carnal appetites. If Matthew Stoner had cared so much for
little Crystal, he wouldn't have brought her to his big, impressive office and tried to seduce her. He was obviously
a reprobate and a lecher. He was a beast for whom hanging
wasn't good enough.

"Well then, Mrs. Adams, if that's settled, perhaps we
should get down to the business at hand." He'd picked up
the cigar and was toying with it, turning it round and round
in his hand as he stared at the brightly glowing tip. "You've
heard of Stephanos Christopoulis, no doubt?"

Unnerved by the quick change of subject, Casey forced
herself to put aside her angry thoughts. Stefanos Christopoulis? What did he have to do with the business at hand?
She shrugged and nodded. "Yes, I've heard of him. Who
hasn't? He's on the cover of some magazine or other at least
once a year. He or one of his girlfriends."

An ironic grin came and went on Matthew Stoner's face.
"Yes, he has an interesting lifestyle." Drawing deeply on
the slender cigar, he turned his chair to gaze out the window.
Spread out below was Boston Harbor with its polyglot of
tugs and tankers, motorboats and cruise ships. Swiveling
back to face Casey, Matthew Stoner cocked his head to one
side and studied her. "I hear you cook a damned good meal,"
he said bluntly.

Casey felt her old confidence returning. She nodded, her
face impassive. She wouldn't react to his crude language.
He just wanted to shock her. And he was jumping from one
subject to another to keep her off balance. She had heard
of businessmen doing this sort of thing. It gave them some

sort of advantage in negotiations—or so they thought. Casey sat back and crossed her legs. Matt Stoner followed her actions, his eyes frankly admiring her legs.

"That's right, Mr. Stoner," Casey said coolly. "I cook a damned good meal." If one could play this game, so could the other—and she could play it as well as Matthew Stoner any day.

"I'd like you to prepare dinner for me next Saturday evening, Mrs. Adams. It will be a small dinner, for four people."

Without being able to stop herself, Casey said the first thing that popped into her head. "Will Crystal be there?"

When she uttered the words, she instantly regretted them. The bitterness in her tone had come through loud and clear. He would think she was a catty woman, when in fact she found his philandering ways reprehensible and could barely contain her dislike of him.

Matthew Stoner appeared unmoved by her question. "She may be. I haven't decided who my dinner partner will be."

"Must be rather like having a stable," Casey murmured dryly. "Or a harem."

He paused before he replied. "I wouldn't know," he said finally. "I've never had either."

Casey looked away. Something in his eyes made her feel ashamed, and that made her angry. Why should she be ashamed of her comment? He deserved it, didn't he?

Lifting her head, Casey met his eyes with her own icy green ones. "I'm afraid I have other plans for next Saturday evening, Mr. Stoner. If you had contacted me earlier, perhaps, but as it is I'm completely booked."

"Cancel them."

"What?" Casey stared at him, not sure she had heard him correctly.

"I said cancel your plans," he repeated, his eyes amused as he watched her expression of outrage.

"I wouldn't cancel them for all the money in the world, Mr. Stoner!" she said haughtily, and began to rise.

"Sit down, Mrs. Adams," he said roughly. "We're not talking about all the money in the world. We're talking about five thousand dollars, for one night's cooking. In addition to your usual fee, of course."

Stunned, Casey settled back into her chair. "How much?"

A satisfied smile crossed Matthew Stoner's face. "I thought that might get your attention."

Anger sizzled in Casey's veins. How dare he imply that she could be seduced by money! "What gets my attention, Mr. Stoner," Casey said coldly, "is your colossal presumptuousness. You seem to think that the whole world revolves around money. You assume that by mentioning an outlandish sum, I'll fall into your lap. Well, you're wrong, Mr. Stoner. I wouldn't work for you for all the money in the world—just as I said a moment ago."

He studied Casey with amused eyes. "Did you know he hates New England cooking?"

Casey looked at him with confusion at the rapid change of subject. "Who does?"

"Stefanos Christopoulis."

"Oh, so we're back to *him* again," she said sarcastically.

"So we are, but then he's the reason you're here."

"Whatever are you talking about?" she asked in exasperation. "You're speaking in riddles." Angrily she rose from her chair and turned to leave. "I don't see any reason to stay—"

"Sit down, Mrs. Adams!" Matthew Stoner's voice lashed across the room like the crack of a whip. A little frightened at the contained violence in his tone, Casey sank weakly back into her chair.

"That's better," he said calmly. "Now at least have the decency to stay and hear me out before you go off in a huff."

Casey summoned up her courage. "Then at least have the decency to speak more plainly."

Matthew Stoner sat forward, his face suddenly all business. Staring at him, Casey once again got the impression of a ruthless pirate. She shivered involuntarily, realizing that he would be a hard man to best in any clash of wills.

"The situation is this, Mrs. Adams. Stefanos Christopoulis and I are involved in delicate negotiations that could have beneficial consequences for both our countries. He was here once last fall and stayed in a local hotel. The entire time he complained about the food, saying it wasn't fit for cattle. We have now reached the stage in our negotiations where he must return for further talks. If all goes well, he'll be coming for an extended stay at my summer home on Cape Cod later in the year. But all must go well, Mrs. Adams. After his last visit, when he complained of indigestion and the poor quality of the food, he almost broke off our talks. I've promised him food that will melt in his mouth next weekend. He's wagered me five thousand dollars that it will be inedible."

He sat back, a grim smile on his face. "If I win, Mrs. Adams, the reason will be you and your cooking. And I'll hand the five thousand over to you with due appreciation." He tapped the ash off his cigar and fixed her with steel-gray eyes. "Are you up for the challenge, Mrs. Adams, or do you want to slink off and admit defeat without even trying to prove yourself?"

Casey leaned back into the comfortable leather chair, her thoughts chaotic. On one hand, she still had the urge to stand up and walk out of this office. Matthew Stoner was an arrogant, domineering bully. And yet what he had just said fascinated her. She felt the pull to her ego and found herself feeling less and less angry at Stoner and more and more intrigued at the possibility of proving Stefanos Christopoulis wrong about Boston cooking.

She looked back at Stoner. "Which hotel did he stay in when he complained about the food?"

Matthew Stoner named a prominent hotel in Boston, one generally well thought of for its food. Casey knew though that anything she prepared would surpass the food they served. In fact, two years ago, she had been offered the position of head chef in their kitchens. She had declined, but it had been a gratifying moment.

Now the idea of satisfying the fastidious appetite of the internationally known Stefanos Christopoulis tantalized her. It had been a long time since Casey had been challenged, and she wasn't one to back down. Stoner had shrewdly recognized that and had appealed to just that part of her.

Casey looked at him again. "Next Saturday evening, you said?"

He nodded. "That's right."

"A dinner for four?"

Again he nodded. "But *you* must be the cook. I don't want any substitutes. You must plan the meal and you must prepare it. That's the only way I'll convince Stefanos to stay and negotiate."

The flattery of that remark wasn't lost on Casey. Stoner had just implied that she was the only person in Boston who could cook a meal that would satisfy the picky palate of Stefanos Christopoulis. It was a heady thought, cooking for a world-famous celebrity and pleasing him—making him, in effect, eat his own words.

A smile flitted across Casey's features. Perhaps she should prepare a breast of crow. . . .

Meeting Matthew Stoner's eyes, Casey decided. "All right, Mr. Stoner, you have yourself a deal."

3

CASEY'S GREEN EYES sparkled as she sailed through Joanie's office and into her own. "You'll never guess who I'm cooking dinner for next weekend!" she said, bending to smell the fresh flowers on a table near the door.

Joanie appeared in the doorway, her face shining with excitement. "Matthew Stoner?"

Casey raised an eyebrow. "You're half right. Matthew Stoner and Stefanos Christopoulis."

"Stefanos Christopoulis!" Joanie clapped her hands together. "Oh, Casey! How wonderful!" She perched herself on a chair by Casey's desk. "Tell me all about it. Everything."

Casey threw off her heavy wool coat and unwrapped a

cashmere scarf from around her neck. "There's not much to tell, Joanie," she said, her eyes dancing with humor. "Matthew Stoner wants me to cook dinner for him and his guests, one of whom will be Stefanos Christopoulis, next weekend. He says that Christopoulis hates Boston food. He claims I'm the only cook in Boston he'd trust to prepare a meal for him." Casey sat down, feeling inordinately pleased. "How's that for a compliment? And by the way, I'll want you to serve. Can you manage a Saturday night away from Dave?"

"*Can* I? Oh, Casey, it's marvelous!" Joanie could barely contain her excitement. "And Matthew Stoner—is everything they say about him true? Is he *really* the sexy hunk the papers claim he is?"

Some of Casey's enthusiasm died. She hesitated a moment, trying to find the right words to explain Matthew Stoner. She couldn't very well admit that he was as sexy, good-looking, and attractive as he was reputed to be. Casey knew him for what he was, after all, and she detested everything he stood for. Yet he was going to be her employer, if only briefly, so it behooved her to be judicious in her comments. She settled on an offhanded, humorous approach.

"He's good-looking, yes," she said, shrugging as if it didn't matter. "And he's very dynamic, but . . . he's not my type at all."

Joanie arched an eyebrow. "Well, well! Pretty picky, aren't we?"

Casey relaxed and grinned. "The trouble with Matthew Stoner is he's too good to be true, and he knows it."

"Oh." Joanie nodded knowingly. "Conceited, eh?"

"Very. The complete egotistical male. I swear he'd seduce a bedpost if there were nothing else around."

Joanie dissolved into laughter. "But I'll bet he'll never be faced with that problem. From all I hear about him, *his* bed will never be empty."

Casey's eyes fluttered away. How true, she thought, remembering the young girl named Crystal. Since leaving Matthew Stoner's office yesterday Casey had been haunted by the vision of him holding Crystal in his arms. No matter how hard she tried to concentrate on the prospect of cooking a meal for Stefanos Christopoulis, the memory of Matthew Stoner passionately kissing the golden-haired girl constantly interrupted. And if that wasn't bad enough, once or twice Casey had even caught herself actually imagining what it would be like to be kissed by him. . . .

Abruptly she stood up and walked to her bookcase. It was filled with cookbooks of every conceivable kind. She took out three of the books and walked back to her desk. Enough of wasting her time thinking about Matthew Stoner. She had a job to do.

"Here's the hard part, Joanie. I've got to come up with a dinner that will not only satisfy Stefanos Christopoulis, but leave him rapturous."

"Oh, that'll be a breeze for you, Casey. I've never seen anyone with such a knack for coming up with luscious menus."

Casey smiled, but inside there was a hard knot of doubt. There was the small matter of five thousand dollars riding on this dinner, not to mention the future of Matthew Stoner's business negotiations with Christopoulis. And somehow Casey didn't think that Stoner would be terribly understanding if her meal wasn't the complete success he expected.

"Oh, by the way," Joanie continued as she opened her notebook, "before I go to the market for vegetables, here are your phone messages. Someone named Cronkite called about a party in April, and Miss Tyrone called. She asked me to have you call her right away." Joanie wrinkled her nose. "She *is* unpleasant, isn't she? You'd think you were talking with the Queen of England at the very least. Only I'll bet the Queen is ten times warmer than good old Pamela."

"Miss Tyrone has a lot to learn about establishing rapport with people, that's for sure," Casey agreed, smiling wryly.

"Sounds like the egotistical Matthew Stoner deserves her," said Joanie as she walked toward the door. She stopped, grinned lopsidedly at Casey, and waggled her fingers in a wave good-bye, then shut the door behind her.

Casey sat and stared at the closed door, struggling with

Joanie's last words. From everything she knew about Matthew Stoner, she should agree with Joanie, but something bothered her about the comment. From somewhere deep inside a protest welled up. Matthew Stoner, seducer of young women, reprobate and cad, still deserved more than that cold fish, Pamela Tyrone.

When Casey dialed the number, Pamela Tyrone answered coolly. "Ah, Mrs. Adams, I've been waiting for your call."

"I just got in, Miss Tyrone. What can I do for you?"

"Matt—er, Mr. Stoner—asked me to call to set up an appointment. Evidently you asked to look over his kitchen."

"That's right. I'll need to look around the kitchen and dining room. No use leaving it to the last minute."

"Of course." Pamela Tyrone's voice communicated subtle disapproval, causing Casey to frown in bewilderment.

"Matt wonders if you could go to his home at four this afternoon," Pamela said, cutting into Casey's puzzled thoughts.

"Four?" Casey checked her calendar. "Yes, four will be fine."

"Good." Pamela gave her Stoner's address. As she wrote it down, Casey noticed that it wasn't very far away. It was probably quite close to the Common, in the elegant Beacon Hill section.

"Fine, Miss Tyrone," Casey said. "Tell Mr. Stoner I'll be there promptly at four."

"I will. And Mrs. Adams . . ."

"Yes?"

"Isn't it a shame that you misunderstood my instructions yesterday afternoon? Mr. Stoner can't *bear* it when visitors bypass me and go straight into his office. And I hear you barged in quite unannounced. I do hope you didn't interrupt any . . . er . . . any delicate negotiations."

Casey's temper began to simmer at the arch tone in Pamela Tyrone's voice. Like hell you do, she thought, but managed a smile and light laugh. "Why, no, Miss Tyrone. Mr. Stoner's guest was just leaving when I arrived. And Mr. Stoner was charm itself. If you hadn't told me he didn't like people barging in, as you put it, I'd never have known. Why, he was as gracious and as welcoming as . . ." Casey seized on an image. "As if he'd been waiting for me all his life."

"Well, isn't that wonderful!" Pamela Tyrone said, false cheer brightening her voice. "I'm *so* glad all went well with you."

Casey frowned again. What was all this about? she wondered. Why did she keep getting the distinct impression that Pamela Tyrone didn't like her? For a moment the suspicion snuck in that Pamela Tyrone was actually glad that Casey had stumbled into Matthew Stoner's office unannounced, but then Casey shook away that thought. No one could be that mean.

After a cordial good-bye, Casey hung up the phone and looked pensively into space. Perhaps everything was in her imagination. Maybe Pamela Tyrone just sounded like she didn't like her. Casey decided she would give her the benefit of the doubt. No use spending any more of her time wondering about it. She'd probably never meet her anyway.

When Casey left her office a little before four, it was snowing. Fat, wet flakes were drifting down from a slate-gray sky, melting as soon as they hit the pavement. It was a typical early-March day in New England. The morning had been brisk and sunny, and now it looked as if a blizzard could be in the offing.

Bundling her coat and scarf around her, Casey hurried to her car. When night fell and the temperature dropped, this snow could very well start accumulating. What was now harmless moisture on the streets could become a treacherous glaze of ice. Casey shivered, remembering just such a time five years ago. She and Andy had been driving home from a Christmas party when a car coming toward them slid on the ice and careened into them. Andy hadn't lived through the night. Ever since the accident Casey had hated winter, hated driving on the snow-covered, icy streets of Boston. Yet she did, if only because she had to. Every spring she heaved a sigh of relief coupled with a feeling of victory.

She had overcome not only her fear, but fierce Father Winter as well.

Matt Stoner's home was an impressive brick townhouse. There were black shutters on the windows and a pineapple-shaped brass door knocker on the shiny black door. Two clay pots containing evergreen shrubs sat on the brick steps leading up to the front door.

As she stood on the steps, Casey was momentarily seized by unexpected apprehension. With stunning clarity she remembered her own childhood home—a green-shingled triple-decker house crammed into a street of similar homes, surrounded by a chain-link fence and cracked sidewalks where weeds and grass valiantly struggled to live. The contrast between the mental image and this impeccably maintained townhouse almost sent Casey hurrying back to her car. What was she doing here, in this plush Beacon Hill neighborhood? She was only little Casey O'Connor Adams, from Southie....

Then reason returned and she laughed away her momentary doubts. No longer. Now she was *the* Casey Adams, rich and successful, and as at home on Beacon Hill as if she were born here. Seizing the knocker, she rapped smartly on the door. The sound echoed in the almost empty street, then the door swung open. A gray-haired woman stood in the doorway, a welcoming smile on her blatantly Irish features. "May I help you?"

Casey returned the smile, feeling suddenly at ease. "I'm Casey Adams. Mr. Stoner is expecting me at four, I believe."

"Oh yes, Mrs. Adams, please come in. I'm Mary O'Reilly, Mr. Stoner's housekeeper." She peered out at the drifting flakes. "I do hope it doesn't get worse. Is spring *ever* going to come?"

"It does seem like it's been winter forever, doesn't it?"

"Oh my, yes! And it seems to get worse every year. When I was a child I loved winter. Now I dread it, can't wait for it to go by."

"That's funny. I was just thinking the same thing as I drove over here."

"I always put it down to old age," the housekeeper said, taking Casey's coat and hanging it in the closet. "But seeing you, I guess I can't blame it on that anymore."

Casey laughed, warmed as much by the woman's easy chatter as by the room she had entered. The hall had been formal, with high ceilings, an oriental rug on gleaming floors, and a dramatic circular staircase that soared toward the upper floors. By contrast, this room with its crackling fire, was a haven of cheery comfort. A painting of a fox hunt hung over the mantle, its rich burgundies and dark greens reflected in the colors of the room. There was a forest-green velvet Chippendale sofa in front of the fireplace and a dark red-cordovan wing chair next to it. On the floor was a well-worn oriental carpet of deep greens, burgundies, and tobacco brown. Brass lamps with dark-tan parchment shades sat on antique cherrywood tables, casting pools of amber light that added to the warmth of the room.

As Casey admired the room, a calico cat, which had been curled up on an afghan on one end of the couch, sat up and yawned with sleepy-eyed satisfaction. "Oh, aren't you beautiful," Casey murmured, leaning over to stroke its silky fur.

"That's Tartan," Mary O'Reilly said. "I keep telling Mr. Stoner that Tatters would be a better name, or Rags, but he insists on Tartan. Says she reminds him of a Scottish plaid."

"She does!" said Casey, smiling. "A lovely, warm Scottish plaid that just goes with this beautiful room."

"I'm glad you like them, Mrs. Adams—the room *and* the cat." Casey whirled at the sound of the deep voice.

Matthew Stoner was standing in the doorway, his suit jacket slung over one shoulder, his tie loosened, and his top shirt button undone. Seeing him there, outlined in the door opening, Casey thought he was the most attractive man she had ever known. Everything in her body seemed to want to reach out to him, as if she were being drawn to a warming flame.

"Good afternoon, Mr. Stoner. I hadn't realized you were there." Casey's eyes fluttered past him to see the housekeeper disappearing down the hall.

"You were too busy with my cat, I guess," he grinned.

"Your cat and your lovely home," Casey murmured, hoping he wouldn't grin at her again. It made it difficult to remember that she didn't like him.

He threw his jacket over the back of the couch and walked toward a long cherry table that served as a bar. Irish crystal sparkled on sterling-silver trays, and the crystal decanters filled with richly-colored liquors were aglow with the warm light. He picked up a decanter and removed the stopper.

"Sherry?" he asked, pouring out some of the golden liquid into a cut-crystal sherry glass.

Casey hesitated. Her first impulse was to say yes, and then sink down onto the velvet couch and sip the smooth wine and let the fire warm her. But she was here on business. She had to remember that.

"No, thank you. I'm here on business." As soon as she said it, she realized how stiff she sounded.

Matt threw her an amused look that set her pulses throbbing. "So you are, but that doesn't rule out a small glass of warming sherry, does it?" He glanced toward the windows that overlooked the street. "It's a real blustery day. Makes you feel like it's January instead of March. How about it?" He held up a glass. "Just a small one?"

"All right," she relented. "But very small."

Watching him pour another glass of sherry, Casey felt the powerful pull of his virility. Even dressed in a three-piece suit he exuded masculinity, as if under that cool, cosmopolitan exterior there was a man whose passions ran high, a throwback to the tough, hardy men who had settled this nation. There was nothing soft about him, from the muscles that rippled under his expertly tailored shirt to the flat, hard stomach that showed no hint of too much drinking or good food. He turned toward her when he finished pouring the sherry, and Casey looked away quickly. Somehow she had the feeling that Matthew Stoner could read faces, and she was afraid of what might be written on hers.

"Have you decided on a menu, Mrs. Adams?" he asked, holding the glass out to her.

"No, I haven't." She couldn't quite meet his eyes. His gaze was much too disconcerting, taking her mind off business and putting it squarely on pleasure. She sank down onto the couch and sipped the sherry. "I've been toying with all sorts of possibilities, but haven't decided on anything definite." Looking up, she found his eyes on her. A sudden shaft of pleasure pierced her, and she trembled as she stared into his smoky eyes. Setting down the glass, Casey forced herself to concentrate on the fire. How very odd. She must find out what kind of sherry he served. She had barely sipped it, yet already it was affecting her.

"But you *will* come up with something, I trust," he was saying.

"What?" Casey looked up quickly and then remembered the trend of the conversation. "Oh! Oh, of course. It's just taking me some time, that's all. I want it to be a perfect dinner. Absolutely perfect."

"Yes, so do I," he murmured, sitting down and stretching out his muscular legs in front of him. Idly he swirled the sherry in his glass. Casey stared at him, transfixed, her emerald eyes caught in a kind of magic spell. He lifted his glass to his lips and his eyes met hers over the rim. Instantly Casey felt the room begin to whirl around her. There seemed to be nothing stable in the world but those gray eyes, mesmerizing her, looking into her soul.

Confused, she looked back to the fire, feeling her cheeks grow hot. Perhaps she should move away from the fireplace. She hadn't noticed how warm it was when she first came into the room. Only after Matthew Stoner appeared had she begun to feel her cheeks glowing.

"What happened to your husband, Mrs. Adams?" The personal question startled Casey out of her reverie, and she stared wordlessly at him for a moment.

"Andy?" she said vaguely, not certain why her employer, this man she barely knew and scarcely cared for, would want to know about her husband. She shifted her gaze back to the fire. "He . . . um." She hesitated, took a deep breath, then looked directly into Matthew Stoner's unreadable eyes. "Andy died in a car accident five years ago. It was after his death that I started my business."

His only reaction was a hint of compassion that flickered

across his face. "I'm sorry to hear that," he finally responded. "You appear to have recovered nicely."

For a moment anger at this unsympathetic comment flared in Casey, then she realized Matthew Stoner had meant no offense. He had merely stated the obvious. She had "recovered" from Andy's death, if devoting all of her energies to her work and avoiding serious involvement with any man could be called that. And sometimes waking in the night in her lonely bed, aching for a man's touch . . .

Casey tried to halt her train of thought, but the smooth sherry, the luxurious room, and the warm fire were enveloping her again. She felt herself drifting in a sensuous haze.

Casey stood abruptly. "I should go to see the kitchen before I get too comfortable here."

Matthew Stoner's gray eyes seemed to smolder. "And what would be wrong with getting comfortable here, Mrs. Adams?" he mused, his voice reaching out across the room to wrap her in warmth.

She took a deep breath. Suddenly her heart was hammering in her breast, her pulse pounding in her ears. She felt weak and giddy, and for a crazy moment wondered what it would be like if Matthew Stoner took her in his arms.

But that wasn't going to happen. Despite his potent magnetism, Stoner wasn't the kind of man for Casey. She knew all about him. She had stumbled upon him in the act of seducing another woman. He probably wrote up his conquests in a little black book, keeping tabs the way a gambler does of his pots won.

Drawing herself up, Casey forced a jaunty smile on her face. "There's only one thing wrong with getting too comfortable, Mr. Stoner. If I do, I'll never get out to the kitchen, where I belong." Turning her back on him she walked toward the door. "Don't bother to get up. I'll find my way on my own."

One corner of his mouth lifted in a grin. "You really are the self-sufficient little woman, aren't you, Casey Adams?"

Knowing that she had to fight the crazy attraction she

felt for him, Casey lifted her chin and turned cool green eyes toward him.

"Very self-sufficient," she affirmed, and closed the door behind her.

4

CASEY PAUSED IN the hallway and took a deep breath to steady herself. How absurd! What was the matter with her? She was acting like a silly schoolgirl, her cheeks hot and her stomach a mass of warm flutterings.

Shaking her head at herself in exasperation, she went in search of the dining room. Yet Matthew Stoner's words seemed to follow her, mocking her. *You really are the self-sufficient little woman, aren't you, Casey Adams?*

For a fearful moment she wondered if he had guessed. Could he have seen through her cool, unruffled exterior to the butterflies that had invaded her stomach? Could he have somehow known that she had been filled with a rush of yearning? Did it show in her face or posture?

Sitting in the comfortable room she had felt like ice cream beginning to melt. Suddenly her hard, squared edges felt smoother, softer, more pliable. If she had stayed in the room, allowed herself to relax more, would she have melted right into his arms—dessert for Matthew Stoner?

Irritated at herself for such fantasies, Casey brusquely lifted her hand and swiped at an imaginary thread on her immaculate sleeve. It would do no good to dwell on her reactions to Matthew Stoner. He was an attractive man and she was a woman. It was inevitable that some day she would meet a man who appealed to her. How ironic that he turned out to be a rogue, the kind of man mothers warned their daughters about. Thank goodness she had seen him in action. The picture of him holding Crystal in his arms was firmly etched in her mind. She needed no other warning to steer clear of him. There would be no foolish infatuation, no dreamy-eyed fantasies of love and living happily ever after. She had known the real thing once, and wasn't going to settle for a sham love affair with her doing all the giving and Matthew Stoner all the taking. That way led to tears on her pillow late at night and a broken heart. It was better to make the boundaries clear right away. He was her client and nothing else. She would keep their relationship on a strictly business level and ignore these small ripples of pleasure that had momentarily marred the placid surface of her life.

In fact, she had begun to do just that. By leaving the room when she did, by cutting off the possibility of a man–woman relationship developing, she had made her position clear. She was working for Matthew Stoner, and that was all.

Satisfied that she was thinking clearly, Casey tried a door that led from the hall. Sticking her head inside, she saw it was the dining room. She opened the door wider and stepped in, shutting the door softly behind her.

The room was as quiet as a deserted church. A thick oriental rug muffled her footsteps, contributing to the churchlike effect. Pale light filtered through French doors from an outside terrace, making the room seem ghostly.

Reaching out, Casey flicked a switch. Immediately the room was filled with light from a large brass chandelier that hung over the massive dining table. Warming rays reflected off the polished surface of the table and glowed among the jeweled tones of the carpet and the dark-red Colonial-pattern wallpaper and matching draperies. Chippendale chairs circled the table, their seats upholstered in the same pattern as the wallpaper and draperies.

Casey wandered to the French doors and looked out. The snow was falling gently from the darkening sky, hitting the uneven brick surface of the terrace and forming puddles that reflected the lights from the dining room. An ivy-covered brick wall surrounded the terrace, creating the impression of a world enclosed and safe, cut off from the houses beyond.

Turning back to face the room, she saw that there was a formal fireplace with a white mantle and a grate filled with birch logs. Her practiced eye swept the room, envisioning it with the table set for a formal dinner and a fire crackling in the fireplace. With the lights dimmed and candles flickering on the shining table, it would be a warm, inviting setting, the kind of room in which guests would linger after the meal, content to prolong their coffee and brandy. There would be no rush to leave, to get back to the more comfortable seats of the living room. Whoever had planned this room had made it as relaxing and inviting as any living room. It was a hostess's dream.

For a brief moment Casey pictured herself seated at one end of the long table. For once she would be the hostess instead of the cook in the kitchen. She would wear a long, green velvet gown. Her shoulders would be bare, and perhaps she would have emeralds at her neck to reflect the green of her eyes and set off sparks against her deep mahogany-colored hair . . .

Casey brought her thoughts up short. This was ridiculous! What was she doing standing in Matthew Stoner's dining room fantasizing about being his hostess? She was here to work for him. Hadn't she just been all through that, realizing there could be nothing between them? These daydreams of hers would have to stop, and the sooner the better. What she needed to do was get down to work, to take inventory of the dining room and kitchen. She would need to see the china, crystal, and silver. She would go through every tablecloth and napkin. When she finished here she would begin in the kitchen, taking stock of every pot and pan, of every whisk and rolling pin. Pulling open a drawer in the china cabinet, Casey set to work, her mind once again unflinchingly on her job.

An hour and a half later she was finished. She had taken extensive notes and felt the stirrings of an idea for the menu. Putting her notebook in her pocketbook, Casey slumped into a kitchen chair. Mary O'Reilly was busy at the stove, her back to Casey. As Casey watched her, Mary turned around and a broad smile appeared on her good-natured face.

"You're all finished, then?" she asked, wiping her hands on her apron.

"All finished." Casey smiled wearily. "It's been a long day. I hope you don't mind that I've collapsed for a moment at your table."

"No hurry, Mrs. Adams. You just stay there and rest. It has been a long day. Would you like a nice, warming bowl of soup before you leave?"

"Oh, I couldn't. Really, I couldn't." Casey sniffed appreciatively. "But it does smell wonderful."

"That settles it then, you'll have a good, hot bowl." Mary O'Reilly began ladling soup from the kettle on the stove, chattering easily. "No use going out anyway. Miss Tyrone says the streets are a mess. The snow has turned to ice and the traffic is at a standstill."

"Miss Tyrone?" Casey sat up. "Did she just call?"

"Call? No, she's here! She showed up a little while ago." A decided frown appeared on Mary's face. "She and Mr. Stoner have some *business* to conduct tonight, it appears," she said, placing an ironic emphasis on *business*. She shook her head and walked carefully toward Casey, a full and steaming bowl of soup in her hands. "Ever since he hired her, she's found more work for him to do after hours than any other secretary I've ever known." Mary put the bowl down, whisked out a spoon and linen napkin from a drawer, then stood before Casey, hands on her hips, a knowing look on her face. "Mr. Stoner feels that's evidence of her devotion to duty." The last three words came out with a heavy underlining of sarcasm.

Casey picked up her spoon and dipped it in the soup. "And you don't?" she asked, trying not to sound too interested.

"Oh, it's devotion, all right—but not necessarily to duty."

Casey fought a smile. It was evident that Mary thought no more of Pamela Tyrone than Casey herself did. "Has she worked for Mr. Stoner long?"

"About six months or so, I'd say. Long enough to make herself indispensable."

"She sounds very efficient."

"Oh, she's certainly efficient. Efficient at sniffing out rich, eligible bachelors."

Casey decided to sample the soup. If she wanted to maintain an open mind about Pamela Tyrone, she'd better not encourage confidences from Mary.

Taking a sip of the soup, Casey forgot all about Pamela. "Mmmm. . . ." She looked up at Mary appreciatively. "This *is* good."

A look of pure joy crossed Mary's face. "Well, I do make a good soup, if I do say so myself," she said, her face reddening. She wiped her hands on her apron like a small child receiving an unaccustomed compliment.

"Who taught you to cook?" Casey asked.

"My mother."

"Me too. We used to spend all day Saturday in the kitchen, experimenting. When Dad was alive, Mom had to stick to meat and potatoes, but she kept telling me I was learning the basics. She taught me to bake bread, biscuits, and cakes from scratch. After Dad died, she branched out. She'd go to a bookstore and buy herself a new cookbook, and we'd plan what to try next." Casey smiled gently, lost in her memories. "It was a good time. . . ."

Mary nodded understandingly, then looked at her watch

and bustled back to the stove. "They'll be wanting dinner any minute."

Casey concentrated again on the soup, but was interrupted when the kitchen door swung open. She looked up to see who had entered, and Mary O'Reilly spun around at the same time. A woman stood in the doorway, looking first at Mary and then at Casey.

Casey was struck by the woman's extraordinary beauty, then by the coldness of her eyes. Icy-blue eyes, like a glacier.

"You must be the famous Mrs. Adams," the woman said, and Casey knew her immediately from her voice. Pamela Tyrone.

Casey stood up and extended her hand. "That's right. And you're Pamela Tyrone."

The hand that took Casey's was slim and cold, as if she had just come in from outside. Pamela looked at the half-finished bowl of soup. "How interesting. I was under the impression that *you* did the cooking, Mrs. Adams." She looked at Mary meaningfully, as if she had caught the housekeeper doing something wrong.

"Generally I do," Casey said, smiling warmly. "But every once in a while I'm lucky enough to enjoy a fellow cook's creation." She refused to be ruffled by this woman. And she would do her best to defend Mary, who was suddenly looking worried. "Have you had the pleasure of sampling Mary's soup?" she continued, taking her seat again. "It's really very good."

"That's why I'm in here, Mrs. Adams, to tell Mrs. O'Reilly that Mr. Stoner and I are ready for dinner." One sleek eyebrow arched over a glacial blue eye. "I'm afraid that's the extent of my acquaintance with the kitchen." Airily she waved in the direction of Mary. "I just leave it all to the hired help and get on with the important work." With a dazzling smile, she pivoted and left the room.

Casey glanced at Mary, whose face mirrored her feelings. Sniffing disdainfully, Mary arched her own thick, graying eyebrow. "Sometimes she forgets that she's also the hired help," she muttered angrily, then started flinging pots and pans around loudly as she readied the meal.

Casey thoughtfully sipped at the rest of her soup. There were all kinds of undercurrents flying around the room. Mary O'Reilly didn't like Pamela Tyrone. Pamela didn't like Mary. And from the little she had seen, Casey once again got the distinct impression that Pamela also didn't like *her*.

One thing was certain—Pamela Tyrone was beautiful. No wonder Matthew Stoner had hired her. As a connoisseur of women, he would naturally want only the most beautiful around him, even in his office. He had probably looked high and low to find her. From Casey's experience, Pamela wasn't an ordinary secretary. She had the refined looks of a socialite coupled with the lanky grace of a fashion model. Her clothes showed off a perfect figure. Her dark, sultry complexion was flawless. Her hair was inky black and pulled back into a severe chignon. That style might have been unbecoming on most women, but it only highlighted Pamela's dramatic looks. And even though she was slim, there was a lushness to her figure, from her thrusting bosom to her wide hips and long, silky legs.

Sexy was the word to describe Pamela Tyrone, Casey decided glumly. Pamela Tyrone was sexy. And beautiful. And desirable. And cold as ice. . . .

The clatter of pots and pans was growing louder. Mary was obviously getting angrier by the minute. A tiny blue cloud seemed to have settled over her gray head, and her movements were stilted and jerky, as if she were barely able to contain her temper. Casey decided it was time to leave. If there was going to be an explosion, she didn't want to be a part of it. Rising from her chair, she carried her bowl to the sink.

"The soup was wonderful, Mary," she said gently.

A smile broke through Mary's clouds for a moment. "Thank you, Mrs. Adams. That's the only thanks I'll get around *here* tonight. Aside from Mr. Stoner's, of course."

Casey looked away, not knowing what to say. If she

commiserated, it would look like she was taking sides. And she *was*. She sided with Mary, understanding what it must be like to be ignored and looked down on by another member of Matthew Stoner's staff. But all the same, it wasn't her place to show how she felt. She settled on a warm smile.

"I appreciate your thoughtfulness, Mary. You've been a great help. I'll see you next Saturday."

"Yes, Mrs. Adams, next Saturday."

In the hall, Casey met up with Matthew Stoner and Pamela as they were leaving the study.

"Leaving already, Mrs. Adams?" Matthew Stoner asked.

"Yes, I've finished my inventory and now all I have to do is sit down, plan the menu, then begin ordering the food." She hesitated. "I may need to speak with you once more before next Saturday. I'll want you to approve the menu. I wouldn't want to serve anything you don't care for."

"Whenever you say, Mrs. Adams, but Miss Tyrone here can take care of all that." He put a hand on Pamela's arm and drew her closer. "Have you met my secretary?"

"Yes, we met just now in the kitchen." Casey smiled at Pamela, whose eyes, for some reason, didn't appear as cold as they had. It was like seeing a twin sister. This Pamela was warmer, more appealing. Friendliness even shone in her eyes.

Pamela cast an amused sideways glance at her employer. "Does Mrs. Adams know that in a roundabout way I'm responsible for her getting this job?"

Startled by this amazing piece of news, Casey looked from Pamela to Stoner in confusion. He grinned. "I don't believe she does," he replied, then went on to explain. "When I was in Pam's office on Monday, I spied the article on you in the Sunday paper. Pam had been reading it and had left it on her desk." A self-mocking grin came and went on his chiseled lips. "I *should* say I spied your picture, but I have a hunch you're the kind of woman who wants to be wanted for her skills and not her feminine attributes." That grin flickered at the corners of his mouth again. "Am I right?"

Casey focused on the painting over his left shoulder,

wondering why she should find his remark oddly comforting. In a roundabout way he was admitting that he liked the way she looked, and that pleased her. His slight teasing hadn't angered her the way it might have a day or two ago. Instead, incredibly, it brought a surge of warmth to her veins, heating the surface of her skin in a pleasant blush. She warned herself that he was just trying out his practiced charm on yet another hapless female, but she didn't care. She shifted her gaze from the painting to his craggy features. Some sort of chemistry pulled her toward Matthew Stoner, despite her conscious knowledge that she should beware of him. He was like a powerful drug, addicting and dangerous. And she knew that even now her eyes were mirroring the warmth she was feeling. She knew she had to look away from those smoky gray eyes, lest he see the attraction she felt for him. Pulling her eyes from his, she caught the displeasure that flashed across Pamela Tyrone's face. And suddenly it hit Casey why Pamela Tyrone might have developed a dislike for her, sight unseen. For it hadn't been sight unseen—Casey's picture had been in Sunday's paper. Perhaps there was something in the article that had struck Pamela the wrong way. Casey would have to reread it to see what it could have been.

In control of herself again, Casey extended a hand to Stoner and smiled. "It's been a pleasure going through your home, Mr. Stoner. It will make a lovely setting for the dinner next Saturday."

"I'm glad you like it." His hand grasped hers, enveloping it in warmth. Casey felt a delightful tingle at the contact, but immediately pulled her hand away. Pamela Tyrone was watching them, her eyes cold once again.

"Well, I'll just get my coat," Casey said lamely, but didn't move. She seemed rooted to the spot, once again drawn to Matthew Stoner, mesmerized by the smoke in his eyes.

"My coat," she repeated, her voice no more than a whisper.

He was looking down at her with steady concentration, not letting her eyes leave his. "What about your coat?" he asked, his voice so low that she could barely hear him.

Her heart was doing strange things, and she felt as if she were quivering inside. She had to force her mind to think. "I'll need it," she said, feeling foolish and silly. "I'm leaving, remember?"

"Ah, yes . . . your coat." His eyes were smiling at her, warming her, making her feel alive and glowing. "I'll get it for you." He walked to the closet and back in a few seconds, holding out the coat for her. She slipped her arms into the sleeves, vivedly aware of his nearness. He smelled totally masculine, a combined scent of aftershave, cigar smoke, and sherry. Her stomach quivered, and it was all she could do to keep herself from turning and sliding her arms around him. She wanted to be held by him, to be pressed close to his hard form and enveloped in his distinctive aroma, caress the wiry hairs that grew on his chest, to feel the scratch of his beard on her skin, to savor his lips, explore his body.

Trembling, she did none of that. Instead, she pulled her collar up and held it close to her throat, as if she could ward off his attractiveness that way. "Thank you again, Mr. Stoner," she managed to say, her voice small and feathery.

A grin twisted one corner of his mouth. "For what, Mrs. Adams?"

Casey's eyes fluttered away from his amused ones, but an answering smile appeared on her own lips. "For the sherry, of course. And the pleasant conversation." Her eyes traveled upward to his while she added the unspoken words. And for making me feel alive again. And beautiful. Desirable. For making my heart trip over itself and my stomach flip-flop when I look at you. For making me feel as if I'm melting inside.

It was delicious to be near a man who was so totally male, to know he was as affected by her femininity as she was by his masculinity. It was something she hadn't experienced in five years, and she was darned if she would cut it short.

His voice seemed to reach out to embrace her. "Be careful outside, Mrs. Adams. I hear the roads are treacherous."

She heard the words, but she didn't hear them. It was like being in a magic spell, bewitched. She was awake, conscious, but not in command. Her senses seemed to have taken over from her brain, telling her to stay with this man, to look into those smoldering gray eyes and respond to him as a woman.

"Forget being a businesswoman," a small voice told her. *"This* is what life is all about—this magic chemistry, this excitement, this hammering in the bloodstream, this hunger—"

But her thoughts were cut short by Pamela Tyrone's discreet clearing of her throat. "Matt? Perhaps we shouldn't keep Mrs. Adams any longer."

The spell was shattered. Casey looked away. Matt's eyes lost their warmth. He cleared his throat and glanced at Pamela, then forced Casey to meet his gaze once again.

"You'll be all right on the roads?" he asked, his eyes searching hers.

"Yes, of course." She smiled jauntily, hearing another, saner voice now. "Fool! You almost forgot! You almost lost yourself in your silly dreams! He's your *client,* remember? Nothing else. *Nothing."*

Casey buttoned her coat quickly, her fingers feeling suddenly stiff and awkward. "Until next Saturday, Mr. Stoner."

He nodded gravely. "Until next Saturday, Mrs. Adams."

She turned away and opened the front door. A cold blast of air hit her, momentarily stunning her with its force. Hesitating on the threshold, she was propelled forward by that same, sane voice of reason. "Get out. Get out, you fool! Leave Matthew Stoner to his luscious secretary. He's not for you."

Chased by the voice of reason, Casey stepped out onto the brick steps. When her foot came into contact with the top step, it flew out from under her.

Ice! she realized with shock, then she was tumbling down the steps.

For a moment there was no coherent thought, then she was aware she was lying on the cold hard steps, her head aching from its precipitous contact with the threshold. She struggled to get up, to get her world back in order and stop it from whirling, but was abruptly enveloped in warmth. She looked up to find Matthew Stoner's gray eyes filled with concern. His arms were strong around her, his hands supporting her head.

"Casey, are you all right?"

She stared at his face, so close to hers, so anxious. A silly smile gathered on her face. Laying her head against his chest, she felt her fingers curling inside her gloves, like kittens snuggling beside a fire.

"Matt," she whispered, feeling strangely warm and safe, "you warned me about the roads, but didn't say a thing about the steps."

Then she was conscious of being lifted, of Matthew Stoner swinging her around and bringing her inside the house, of being cherished, and then everything went blank.

5

"I'M ALL RIGHT, I tell you. Really I am." Casey sat up in the huge, canopied bed, her protests falling on deaf ears.

"You'll stay where Mr. Stoner put you," Mary O'Reilly commanded. "You hit your head and blacked out. Mr. Stoner's calling the doctor now."

"But that's absurd!" Casey swung her legs over the side of the bed and slid to the floor. "A little bump on the head and Matthew Stoner will have me going in for brain surgery if I'm not careful." Casey's fingers trembled as she buttoned her blouse. She wanted to ask who had undressed her, but she didn't dare. It couldn't have been Matt...or could it have been? She hesitated as she zipped her skirt. Had she dreamed it, or had Matthew Stoner kissed her as he carried her to this room? The memory was fuzzy, but she felt her heart lurch and her skin seem to vibrate with the memory of masculine lips grazing her cheek. He had placed her on the bed and her eyes had fluttered open. They had stared at each other, and then—was it a *dream?*—his lips had closed over hers. Her mouth had opened sensuously at his touch, her tongue becoming entangled in his as her fingers moved over his muscled chest, seeking the buttons, searching for a way inside his shirt, to feel the warmth of his hair-roughened skin. . . .

But everything went blank after that. And now, dressed once again, her fingers trembled as she touched her lips. Had he kissed her? And had she responded so wantonly? Hot color surged into her cheeks. If so, how could she face him?

But there was no time to prepare her chaotic thoughts. A rough, masculine voice lashed out at her from the doorway. "What are you doing, Mrs. Adams? Have you completely lost your senses?"

She whirled around to find Matthew Stoner bearing down on her, an angry scowl on his face. "I'm getting dressed, Mr. Stoner," she said, lifting her chin defiantly. Of course she hadn't kissed him! How absurd of her to think she had! She didn't even like the man! "I appreciate your concern, but I'm fine. I'm going home now. Believe me, I'm perfectly all right."

"You're not going anywhere but back to bed. Take off those damned clothes."

Her flashing eyes challenged his stormy gray ones. "I'm not one of your girlfriends, Mr. Stoner, to order around as you wish." They stood staring at each other, eyes warring, and then somehow the atmosphere around them altered subtly, taking on an electric charge. The expression in his eyes changed, frank assessment replacing the anger.

"If you don't take off those clothes, Mrs. Adams," he warned softly, "I'll do it for you. I assure you I've had plenty of experience."

"I'm sure you have, sir," she answered, pleased that she

didn't blush. "But in much different circumstances, I assume. Or do you have to hit your women over the head to get them into bed with you?"

"My women, Mrs. Adams?" he asked, sounding dangerous.

Casey looked around for Mary O'Reilly, suddenly feeling the need for protection, but she realized that Mary had slipped out of the room as soon as Stoner appeared.

"You're not answering me, Mrs. Adams. What women were you referring to?"

"All those women you've so much experience undressing. Isn't that obvious, Mr. Stoner?"

A grim smile played at the corners of his mouth. Pulling back the covers of the bed, he gestured for her to get in it. "Then leave your clothes on, but get in this bed. The doctor's on his way."

"In this weather?" Casey's anger was simmering again. "Good heavens, I slipped and hit my head. You'd think it was something major."

"And so it would be with any normal head. It appears I don't have to worry any longer. Yours is as hard as those bricks you hit." His eyes gleamed at her. "Maybe I should check my front steps, call in a mason for repairs, perhaps."

"I didn't hit the bricks, Mr. Stoner," she corrected him. "I hit the threshold."

"Ah, then at the very least I'll need a competent carpenter. Structural damage may have resulted."

Laughter trembled on her unwilling lips. "And you're afraid your house may come tumbling down?"

"Something like that." He took her arm. "Now in the bed you go, like a good girl."

She glared at him, unreasonably furious at his tone. How dare he treat her like a child! Would he take that patronizing tone with Pamela Tyrone? Casey tore her arm from his grasp and climbed onto the bed, indignant. "You're being silly. This is all out of proportion to what happened. I'm perfectly fine. Not even a headache."

"That will come later, I'm told."

"By whom? That witch doctor you consulted?"

He grinned amiably. "Why are you so angry with me? I'm only looking after your welfare."

She snorted. "I'd venture that you're more concerned with a suit against your insurance."

"My dear Mrs. Adams, you malign me." He continued grinning at her while he took a seat on the edge of the bed. Casey moved as far away as possible. She knew she was being unreasonable, but didn't take the time to figure out why. He had made her angry, and she couldn't even remember now what he had said to anger her. She was relishing it though. There was something free about it, something unlike her usual calm composure. She felt unconfined, free. Yes, that was it—she felt *alive!*

Matthew Stoner was grinning devilishly, apparently amused by a private joke. She glared at him. "Well?" she demanded. "What's so funny?"

"I was just thinking what will happen when word gets around that Casey Adams spoiled my dinner." He raised a mocking eyebrow. "Your reputation will be in ruins."

"Not so much as when everyone hears that you carried me up to your bed," she snapped.

He laughed softly. "Not my bed, I'm afraid. Merely a guest room."

She glanced around the room, noting the fine antiques and thick carpeting. "I should have known. Yours must be heart-shaped with mirrors suspended above it."

He shook his head. "No. Actually, I'm into whips."

Startled, she could only stare at him, feeling the color creeping up her neck and into her face. The look of satisfied amusement on his face infuriated her. Clenching her jaw, she lay back on the pillows. The first indication of a headache was appearing as a dull pounding in the back of her head.

"Did I offend you, Mrs. Adams?"

"All crude people offend me, Mr. Stoner." She winced as she put a hand to her head. "You don't have any aspirin, do you?"

The amusement left his face. "So you are in pain."

"A little." She shrugged, not liking the bleak, I-told-you-so look in his gray eyes. "I'll live, I'm sure."

"You'd better. I've got five thousand dollars riding on you."

She smiled cheerfully. "Well, I'm glad to know the real reason for your concern. For a moment there I actually thought you *cared* whether I split my head open or not."

"*That* head?" His teeth flashed in a mocking grin as he stood up. "I'll just go check to see if the doctor's arrived."

"While you're at it, check the threshold, too," Casey muttered sarcastically.

"I'll send the doctor up when he arrives. Try not to be too rude to him, Mrs. Adams. It's a nasty night and he's making a special trip out in it just for you."

"On the contrary, Mr. Stoner," Casey said icily. "He's making the trip for *you*." A momentary, irrational flash of annoyance at his money surged through her. No doctor made house calls any more—except for the very wealthy, of course. She tossed her hair back from her face indignantly, and instantly regretted the action when pain zig-zagged through her head. Doggedly, she refused to let Matthew Stoner see her discomfort. "If I had my way, I'd be going home right now."

"And you'd probably black out again and go off the road and end up getting killed." He grinned. "And then what would I do with Stefanos Christopoulis on Saturday?"

"I see that your concern for me is really self-interest."

"Enlightened self-interest, yes. I'm a good businessman and good businessmen protect their investments."

Casey pinched herself elaborately on the arm. "Am I really flesh and blood? I'm beginning to feel like a stack of bank notes."

His eyes ran over her slender figure. "Very nicely stacked, too."

"I don't know what irritates me more, Mr. Stoner— being treated like an investment or like a tart."

He laughed softly. "I wouldn't know. Tarts are your business, Casey Adams, not mine."

"That's not what all of Boston reads in the gossip columns," she retorted, raising an eyebrow sardonically.

"You shouldn't believe everything you read."

"What about believing what I see with my own eyes?"

Nothing seemed to faze him. He merely grinned that infuriating grin of his and turned off the light. "I'm going downstairs to try to redeem what's left of dinner. Miss Tyrone is waiting with a stack of papers a mile high. If you're smart, you'll take my advice and stay in bed until the doctor arrives."

Casey closed her eyes, hoping he would get the message that she found him boring. "If *you're* smart, Mr. Stoner, you'll just leave."

That soft laugh again. "Pleasant dreams, Mrs. Adams," he said, then closed the door quietly behind him.

Casey stared up at the canopy that covered the bed. "Pleasant dreams," she thought sarcastically. The only dreams she was likely to have in that maddening man's house were nightmares.

"No concussion, Mrs. Adams. Just a bad bump."

Casey lay in bed the next morning, remembering Dr. Vincent's words. "You're very lucky," he had added. "You must have a hard head."

Matthew Stoner had followed the doctor upstairs and stood behind him. At that comment he had raised his eyebrows at her in mock astonishment. "Casey Adams?" he seemed to be saying. "A hard head?"

Casey gave him a venomous look, and soon he left her alone with the doctor, who had given her some pills that had not only cured her headache, but had put her to sleep in record time.

Now the morning sun spilled through the window and Casey lay still, listening to the melting snow splashing in the gutters outside. Whenever a car went by, she could hear the *whish* of tires on the wet streets. The storm had gone and spring had come.

Slipping out of bed, she went to the window and saw that the snow was melting in patches. It lay on the small area of green lawn like a lace shawl on a green dress.

The door opened behind her, and Mary O'Reilly poked her head in. "So, you're awake. Feeling better?"

"Much," Casey said, grinning as she looked down at the white shirt of Matthew Stoner's, which she had used as a nightgown. "But feeling a little foolish, also. I've put you to so much trouble."

"Nonsense! You're not any trouble at all. I've got a tray outside with a good, hot breakfast for you. Shall I bring it in?"

"You shouldn't have—but, yes, please do. I'm famished."

"It's good to have a woman in the house who's not afraid of good food." She set the tray on a table near a chaise longue and picked up the silver lid from a steaming plate of scrambled eggs, bacon, and English muffins. "Whenever Miss Tyrone stays overnight, she only has a sip of tea and a piece of dry toast for breakfast." Mary made a face. "Watching her figure, she always says."

Casey stared at the appetizing food, hardly seeing it. "Oh. I see." She picked up her fork and played with the eggs, trying not to appear too interested. "Does she stay here often?"

Mary shrugged. "At least once a week. They work late, and Mr. Stoner doesn't like her going home alone so late at night, so he asks her to stay."

Casey forced herself to take a bite of the eggs. "How nice of him," she murmured, feeling murderous rage engulf her. The lecher! she thought. Swine. Libertine. Womanizer. Looking up at Mary, she smiled sweetly. "This tastes wonderful!" As Mary beamed, Casey simmered. How could she have allowed herself to be attracted to him? she asked herself hotly. Wasn't it enough that she had walked in on him in his office while he was seducing a child young enough to be his own daughter? Did she need this, too? To find out that his secretary was probably his mistress?

"Is something wrong, Mrs. Adams. Aren't the eggs cooked completely?"

Casey had forgotten Mary. "What?" She looked up. "Oh. The eggs." She smiled widely, dispelling Mary's concerned expression. "They're just fine, Mary. Why do you ask?"

"The look on your face. You looked . . ."

Casey shook her head dismissingly. "Pay no mind, Mary. I was just remembering all the things I have to do today."

Mary retreated backward, relief evident in her smile. "Then I'll get back to the kitchen. I'm glad you're feeling better, Mrs. Adams."

"Yes, Mary, thank you." Casey sat and stared at the door after it closed, wondering why she was suddenly so depressed. When she had first awakened she had felt so good. Now she felt as though someone had pulled a gray drapery across the morning sun.

Shrugging, Casey picked up her fork once more. It must be the aftereffects of the medicine the doctor had given her. Yes, that was it. It had to be the medication.

Casey spent the weekend debating about what to serve Stefanos Christopoulis the following Saturday. While taking inventory of Matthew Stoner's kitchen and dining room and seeing the gracious setting—the epitome of New England traditional elegance—she had felt the stirrings of an idea. But the more she thought about it, the more she realized it wouldn't work. It would be a total disaster. Impossible. Christopoulis would hate it.

Yet on Monday morning, when Pamela Tyrone looked up from the menu, Casey was at ease with her decision.

"This is a joke, isn't it?" Pamela asked. "Surely you're not serious."

"Oh, I assure you, I'm very serious." Casey stood her ground as Pamela looked at the menu again, disapproval written all over her face.

"But it's so . . ." Pamela broke off, as if she were unable to find words to describe it. "It's so . . . plain," she finished lamely. "I mean, it's . . . it's . . ."

"Ordinary." Casey supplied the word.

"Yes!" Pamela's face lit up, then darkened again. "Yes.

Unspectacular. Average. Mundane. There's nothing special about it." Her crisp efficiency had returned with full force. "Why, Mary O'Reilly could have come up with this menu. Frankly, Mrs. Adams, I'm rather disappointed in you."

Casey shrugged. "It's the meal I think will work. If you disagree, perhaps you'd better speak with Mr. Stoner."

Pamela toyed with a pen, a calculating look on her face. Watching her, Casey could almost see the cogs and gears spinning in that fertile brain. A look of cunning was quickly replaced by rueful amusement. Pamela handed the menu back to Casey with a pretty shrug. "You're the expert, Mrs. Adams. If you want this, that's what it will be. There's no need to bother Mr. Stoner with the petty details."

Casey felt a momentary flash of anxiety. Pamela was obviously hoping that she would fall flat on her face. Had Casey's instincts been wrong, then? Was this exactly the worst kind of meal to serve in one wealthy man's home to another fabulously rich man? Casey chased the doubts away. No, she had been serving meals to the rich for the past five years and had never misjudged the situation yet. She would stick by her menu. Tucking it back into her briefcase, she turned to go.

Pamela rose from her desk. "Oh, by the way, Mrs. Adams, good luck. Matt told me about the wager."

Casey stopped at the door and looked back. "He did?"

"Yes. He's putting an awful lot of trust in you. I hope it hasn't been misplaced."

Casey thought that a shark's smile would have been friendlier. "I hope not," she replied mildly.

"Well, we'll see on Saturday, won't we?"

"I suppose we will," Casey said, and couldn't resist adding, "It's a pity you won't be there to see firsthand."

Pamela's laughter rang softly, like wind chimes. "Oh, but I will be, Mrs. Adams! Didn't Matt tell you?"

Casey felt her heart sinking to her knees. "Why, no, he didn't mention it."

Pamela looked like a satisfied cat hovering over a trapped canary. "Yes, I'm going to be Matt's hostess Saturday evening. So you see, I'm going to be right there." She paused like a veteran actress who wants to give her lines an extra dramatic thrust. "Matt often asks me to be his hostess, Mrs. Adams. We get along very well, Matt Stoner and I."

6

THE INSISTENT RINGING of the telephone interrupted Casey's dreams. She reached out and groped for the light switch, then sat up in bed, blinking against the sudden brightness.

"Hello?"

"Casey Adams?"

The fog in her brain lifted at the crisp male tone. She knew that voice. . . . "Yes?"

"Matt Stoner. Did I wake you?"

She glanced at the clock and saw that it was a little after eleven. She had gone to bed early in anticipation of the long day tomorrow, preparing the meal for Stefanos Chrisopoulis. "As a matter of fact, you did."

"I would have called earlier, but it took a couple of hours to track you down."

"I keep my number unlisted on purpose, Mr. Stoner— for just this reason." Casey knew he was amused, even though he wasn't laughing out loud. She could almost feel his grin reaching out to her through the receiver. "How did you get my number, by the way?"

"I found out the name of your assistant and looked her up in the phone book. I practically had to throttle her to convince her to give me your number. You won't fire her, will you, for giving out confidential information? I told her it was a matter of life and death."

"Is it?" Casey rested her chin on her knees, smiling in spite of herself.

"Before I tell you, you've got to promise me you won't take it out on your assistant."

"Take what out?" she asked, her smile widening.

"Then you're not angry?"

She shook her head, her eyes laughing. "No, I'm not angry, Mr. Stoner. What's the problem?"

"No problem, Mrs. Adams. I just wanted to know if you're all set for tomorrow."

She sat straight up. "You mean you called me after eleven for *that?*" she asked incredulously. "Do you call the people who work for you to ask them if they're prepared for their meetings the next day?"

He chuckled. "All right, I apologize. I forgot—you're a businesswoman."

"And a darned good one!" she said hotly.

"Okay, Okay. Don't get your temper flaring."

"Is that all you wanted, Mr. Stoner, or was there something else?" Casey lay back down, cradling the receiver against her shoulder. For some inexplicable reason, the image of Matthew Stoner as he had looked in the hallway of his home the other evening came back to her, almost taking her breath away with its potency. Once again she experienced the full shock of his gray eyes on hers and felt her anger slipping away, replaced by the same longing that had filled her then. But even while she wanted to hang on to this feeling, she knew she had to fight it. Matthew Stoner wasn't the kind of man she should be involved with. He was a charmer, out for sheer physical pleasure without any commitment. No matter what messages her body was getting, she was going to do her best to short-circuit them with her intelligence.

"What I need to know, Mrs. Adams, is where you live."

"Oh? What for? Are you doing a last-minute credit check on me?"

"No, I just need to know where to pick you up tomorrow."

"Pick me up? Who said anything about your picking me up? I'm catering a meal for you, Mr. Stoner, not going on a date with you."

"Well, that's very true, Mrs. Adams, but you might be kept late in the kitchen and I wouldn't want you going home alone that late at night. That's why I feel it's best that I pick you up and then take you home at the end of the evening."

She raised an eyebrow. "I assure you, Mr. Stoner, I *am* a big girl. I've been driving by myself for years now, even after dark." Inside, she could feel her temperature rising. That must have been the line he used on Pamela Tyrone when he first seduced her. And speaking of Pamela, how would *she* get home? Or would she stay behind, warming Matthew Stoner's bed until he returned from taking home the hired help?

"Ah, that's right," he said softly. "I almost forgot. You're the independent type."

"Let's just say I don't need a big, strong man to take care of me," she said coolly, and could almost feel his grin splitting his face, even though he wasn't laughing out loud. Anger gritted in her bloodstream like sand, chafing and irritating. But she felt helpless to express it.

"My apologies, Mrs. Adams. Sometimes I forget myself after a day riding around the jungle on a vine."

Despite herself, her lips twitched in humor. He was the

most *galling* man! But he had that mocking humor that kept penetrating her defenses, making her want to laugh.

"Apology accepted," she said grudgingly.

"Good. Now what's your address?"

Exasperated, she sat up and slung her legs over the side of the bed. "I don't *need* you to chaperone me, Mr. Stoner. Believe me, I don't."

"I realize that, Casey. This has nothing to do with my chaperoning you, so don't let your liberated blood boil."

Part of her wanted to stay angry because it was her best defense against him, but another part was thinking about the way her name had sounded on his lips. "Casey." She liked the way he said it, caressingly almost, making her feel warm and feminine and desirable. . . .

"What has it got to do with, Mr. Stoner?" she asked, trying to keep her mind on the conversation and not her body's startling reactions to this man.

"First of all, let's stop this last-name business. Call me Matt."

She closed her eyes as delicious longings flooded over her. Damn the man, he was slipping behind her defenses and she didn't even know how he was doing it! "All right," she agreed. "Matt."

"That's better. The reason I want to take you home, Casey, is that I'm going to need to go over a few things with you after the dinner, and it might take a while."

"What kind of things?"

"First of all, the five thousand dollars—"

"*If* you win the bet," she interrupted.

"Where's your self-confidence?" he teased. "I've got complete faith in you and your cooking."

A pang went through her. What if he didn't like the meal? What if she had taken the wrong approach, made a bad decision? Hesitantly, she broached the subject.

"Did Miss Tyrone tell you what I plan to serve?"

"No, she didn't even mention seeing you. Have you talked with her?"

"Yes, I went around to her office the other day and let

her see the menu." Casey bit at her lip, stalling. "Er, she wasn't very impressed, I'm afraid."

There was a long pause on Matt's end. "Oh?" he said cautiously.

"Yes. In fact, she was rather disappointed. At least I believe that's how she phrased it."

There was another pause, this one slightly more chilly. "What *are* you serving, Mrs. Adams?"

So much for first names, Casey observed wryly. It hadn't taken very long to return to a business footing. "Nothing fancy," she said. "Nothing exotic. Just a plain old American meal."

A third pause. Not a friendly pause. "What? Hot dogs and beans?"

She smiled despite herself. "Not quite that ordinary."

"How ordinary?"

She took a steadying breath. "Clam chowder for the first course, then stuffed scallops, fresh asparagus with lemon butter, wild rice with mushrooms, green salad, a California Chablis, and raspberry sherbet with sugar wafers for dessert." She squeezed her eyes shut and waited for the ax to fall.

He spoke after a moment. "What's wrong with that?"

Her eyes flew open. He wasn't mad! He even sounded pleased. She was vindicated! Her words tumbled over themselves in an effort to get out. "Nothing's wrong with that, or at least that's how I looked at it. Miss Tyrone wanted something fancy, but I figured that Christopoulis had probably objected to the hotel's food because it was the kind that any person could get in any hotel in the world. I thought he'd appreciate an American meal in an American home—"

"Good, that's settled. Now what's your address?"

The persistence of the man! Shaking her head, she grinned wryly. "All right, I'll compromise. I'll have my assistant's boyfriend bring me with her. Then you can take me home. Does that suit you?"

She heard his low laugh and felt a shiver of sensual

awareness feather across her skin.

"It suits me perfectly, Mrs. Adams," he said, and then hung up.

Casey lay back and stared up at the ceiling. Her sleepiness was gone, chased away by an urgency that had invaded her body. She felt alive and strangely aware of everything about herself. She switched off the light, then rolled onto her side, one hand smoothing the flat expanse of bed beside her. Sighing deeply, she thought of smoldering gray eyes . . . of thick, rumpled black hair and a solid, muscular chest . . . of strong arms and long, muscled thighs. It was hours before she got to sleep.

Casey gave the dining room a final inspection, noting the sparkling crystal, the gleaming sterling flatware and serving pieces, the thin tapers ready to be lit in the sterling candelabra. Spring flowers burst from the greenery embedded in a glass-lined sterling Revere bowl. The mingled scents of irises, daffodils, tulips, forsythia, and anemones drifted in the air. Antique scarlet-and-gold Sèvres china sat on an ivory lace tablecloth. A fire had been laid in the fireplace, but the glass doors had been closed to keep the wood smoke from obscuring the smells of food and flowers.

From down the hallway came a muted burst of laughter. Stefanos Christopoulis and his latest mistress, Anna Copeland, were here already. Matt and Pamela were with them, having pre-dinner cocktails in the formal living room. The door opened and Joanie came in, hurrying toward Casey.

"Is everything okay?" Casey asked, falling into step beside her assistant as they entered the kitchen.

"Wonderful!" Joanie's eyes sparkled as she turned to Casey. "Oh, Casey, that Matt Stoner is something else! I've got all I can do to keep from tripping over myself whenever I look at him."

"That's fine, just as long as you don't drop dinner on anyone," Casey said wryly. "How are you going to explain those stars in your eyes when Dave picks you up tonight?"

Joanie shrugged. "It'll do him good to get a little jealous. He's been taking me for granted lately." With a grin, she swept from the kitchen to make her way back to the living room with a platter of hot hors d'oeuvres.

Casey sighed and checked the clock. It was time to finish preparing the meal. From now on, she wouldn't have time to think about anything but her cooking. Putting on an apron, she set to work.

A little over an hour later she looked up as Joanie brought in a tray laden with the bowls that had contained the chowder.

"How's it going?"

Joanie waved a hand dismissingly. "Piece of cake. I've never heard so many ooohs and aaahs in my life."

Casey grinned and turned back to the stove. She hadn't told Joanie that money was riding on this dinner, figuring that the less Joanie knew, the less nervous she would be. As for Casey herself, she was too much the professional to let it bother her. When everything was finished, before she heard the final verdict, she might get a case of nerves, but now she was the complete professional, immersed in her work.

Another hour later she stood leaning against the sink, her arms folded, waiting to hear the final result. Her doubts had resurfaced. The plates had come back empty, but that alone didn't mean they had liked the meal. And most important, what had Stefanos Christopoulis thought?

The dining room door swung open, and Joanie stuck her head in. "Casey?"

Casey's head flew up. "Yes?" She stared at Joanie, feeling her heart skip a beat. Oh no, had something gone wrong?

"Mr. Christopoulis would like to speak to you."

"With me?" Casey moistened her lips. Please let it be all right, she prayed, if not for my sake, then for Matt's.

Joanie gestured frantically. "Come *on!*" she whispered.

Casey looked down at herself. She hadn't bothered to dress up, figuring she would be in the kitchen and no one would see her. She had worn a pair of faded jeans and a loose silk tunic, and had pulled her thick hair back into a ponytail. She yanked the rubber band out and her hair fell around her face in thick waves.

"Is he angry?" she whispered to Joanie at the door.

Joanie gave her a strange look and shoved her into the dining room. Everyone was looking at her. There might be only four guests in the room, but it felt like a hundred. She saw Matt, devastatingly handsome in a dark suit and white shirt, and opposite him, Pamela Tyrone, wearing a low-cut black dress. And Anna Copeland, the famous Hollywood movie star, looking splendid in blue silk.

And Stefanos Christopoulis. His black eyes swept her from head to foot. "But I asked to speak to the chef," he said, his words thick with a Greek accent. "Not the scullery maid."

Casey's professionalism held up. Smiling graciously, and with a touch of humor, she cocked her head to one side. "I am the chef, Mr. Christopoulis. I hope everything was all right."

Christopoulis sat staring at her, his face impassive, his bulky frame appearing out of place in the elegant room.

"I am a poor loser, Miss—" he broke off. "I didn't catch your name."

"Mrs. Adams. Casey Adams."

He nodded, his massive head covered with a tight cap of grizzled gray curls. "Mrs. Casey Adams," he repeated. "As I was saying, I'm a poor loser. And tonight I lost quite a sum of money because of you."

There was a small gasp of surprise from Anna Copeland. Casey darted a quick glance toward Matt, who sat lazily in his chair, a small smile playing on his lips.

"I see," Casey answered cautiously. She thought it was better to pretend ignorance about the bet. "How did that happen?"

He pointed a blunt finger at her. "Because you cook so damned good, that's why!" his voice boomed out. "I had a bet with Matthew that no one in this God-forsaken city could cook a decent meal. You proved me wrong." He patted his chest. "No indigestion either. A bonus!"

Casey was in a quandary. How should she respond? That it was too bad he had lost the bet, or great that he didn't have indigestion? She decided on a compromise.

"Well, I'm sorry about your losing the bet, Mr. Christopoulis, but pleased you like my cooking."

He grunted, looking from Casey to Pamela. "Matthew, how do you get any work done with one beautiful woman in your office and another in your kitchen?"

Matt's teeth flashed in a grin. "Mrs. Adams is here tonight especially for you, Stefanos. She's a caterer." His eyes gleamed as they flicked over her. "I can assure you that if she were in my kitchen on a regular basis, I wouldn't be eating in the dining room."

Casey looked down quickly, but not before noticing the displeasure on Pamela's face. In the general laughter, Casey turned to go.

"Mrs. Adams?"

She turned back to Christopoulis. "Yes?"

"My compliments. The meal was excellent."

She felt triumphant. "Thank you, sir. That means a lot to me." But when she turned to go, she thought there were daggers in Pamela Tyrone's eyes.

Casey had just finished cleaning the counters and was undoing the strings of her apron when the door swung open behind her. She turned to find Matt Stoner standing in front of the closed door, one corner of his virile mouth turned up in a mocking grin. His eyes traveled in a lazy path from her tousled hair down to the silk tunic that molded her breasts, then lowered to the faded jeans that fit her long, slim legs to perfection.

"So this is the now world-famous caterer Casey Adams," he murmured, eyes glittering with amusement. He put a thin cigar to his lips and lit it, puffing out a leisurely stream of smoke. "I think I agree with Stefanos—you look more like a scullery maid."

Temper flared along Casey's nerve endings. Was this the kind of thanks she would get for her efforts? "What did you expect?" she sniped. "That I'd show up in a tall white hat, twirling my moustache?" She bunched up her apron and angrily stuffed it into a canvas satchel. "The point is, Mr. Stoner, that the meal was a success. The chef's looks didn't matter in the least."

"Didn't they?" The words were spoken in a low voice, breathed out with the smoke from the cigar and tinged with amusement and something else, something indefinable but vaguely sexual. Once more Matt's eyes drifted downward. Heat flared in Casey's cheeks so that she was forced to turn away. She felt her heartbeat accelerate. Damn the man! Why did he have such an explosive effect on her? She knew he was a bounder. Why couldn't she fight the attraction she felt for him?

Casey bent down to pick up the canvas tote, slung it over her shoulder, and turned to face him, feeling in a combative mood. If she couldn't fight her feelings, she could at least fight the person who inspired them.

"I'm ready to go, Mr. Stoner. It's been a long day."

He arched a sarcastic eyebrow, leaned back against the counter, and folded his arms. "But we have lots more to discuss, Mrs. Adams."

Maddening. Absolutely maddening. Feigning blasé weariness, Casey held out her hand. "The only thing I want to discuss is my fee. The check, Mr. Stoner. If you please."

"It appears the woman is money mad."

"No, I just like to eat."

The infuriating eyebrow flew up again. "What's your usual diet? Caviar and filet mignon?"

"Only for breakfast," she said dryly, her hand still out, palm up. She rubbed her thumb and fingers together. "The check please, for five thousand five hundred—the amount of the bet plus my usual expenses. I'm tired and I want to go home."

"You don't look tired, Mrs. Adams. Your cheeks are flushed and your eyes are sparkling and you look..." he hesitated, cocking his head to one side and considering her with narrowed eyes. "You look very pretty, Mrs. Adams," he said finally, nodding judiciously. "Very, very pretty."

Again the heat surged through her veins and up into her cheeks. She dropped her hand, slapping the counter in pretended exasperation. "Mr. Stoner, I'm tired. It's been a long day. I'd like my money. Your compliments are nice, but I'd prefer a warm bed right about now."

She heard herself too late. Matt's grin widened, then, at the expression on her face, he threw back his head and laughed out loud.

"Just what I like in a woman, Mrs. Adams. A no-nonsense approach to romance. Forget the compliments and haul me off to bed."

Casey's green eyes narrowed. What he had said was too close for comfort. She drew herself up and fixed him with a murderous look.

"I'll just pretend you didn't say that, Mr. Stoner. It was bad enough coming here to cook for you and your jet-set friends, but sparring with you and your sexual innuendoes is altogether too much." Wearily she pushed a hand back through her thick hair. "I really am tired. Can we go now?"

"No, I'm afraid we can't. When I said we had a lot to discuss, I meant it."

Feeling a little like a disillusioned child, she stared at him with unhappy eyes. "But you said you'd take me home afterward."

With easy grace he pushed away from the counter and took hold of her arm. "So I did, Casey Adams, but I didn't say what time, now did I?"

7

CASEY WAS SUDDENLY vibrantly aware of the broad, masculine chest that loomed so close to her. Her eyes fastened on the buttons that marched down the stiff, white shirt front, but her body was aware of other, more intimate, details. Her senses were filled with Matt Stoner. His warm hand felt strong, almost possessive, on her silk-covered arm. The scent of his aftershave mingled with the smoke from his cigar, sending a shaft of pure sensual pleasure through her. While her eyes saw the buttons on his shirt, her mind insisted on envisioning the hair-roughened chest beneath that shirt.

Taking a deep breath to steady herself, she lifted wary eyes to his strong features and was pierced by pleasure when she saw Matt Stoner's lips curved in wry amusement. She couldn't look away from his mouth. The sweet ache of desire mounted inside her as she stared at his lips. What would it be like to kiss him? Would he be gentle or crush her against him? And what would he taste like?

Casey's eyes burned as she stared at Matt's mouth. She could almost experience it, the feel of those lips on hers, with the mingled tastes of tobacco and wine and fine brandy. Feeling like a puppet, she tilted her head upward, her eyes meeting Matt's in a jolt of recognition. They stood for a moment, their eyes locked on each other, his hand starting to lightly caress her arm. And once again the memory intruded—she *had* kissed him the night she fell. It hadn't been a dream. It couldn't have been. It was too real, too powerful. Too unnerving. . . .

With a sudden flash of fear, Casey tore her gaze away and pulled her arm from his grasp. Reeling, she put the width of the kitchen between them. She tossed her head rebelliously, angry as much at herself for her feelings as she was at Matt for making her feel this way. "Well," she challenged, her chin tilted up defiantly, "what is it you wanted to discuss?"

His lips quirked in amusement. For a moment Casey was afraid he was going to come after her, but then he settled lazily back against the counter opposite her, his eyes filled with laughter. She wished she could lash out at him and slap that knowing look off his arrogant face, but that would mean giving up the safety of her corner and crossing the wide space that separated them, and she couldn't allow herself to do that. It just wasn't safe. And what infuriated her was the knowledge that her own volatile emotions were the danger, not the silently amused man who stood across the room from her.

She tossed her hair back from her face and crossed her arms tightly in front of her. "Well?" she challenged again. "Cat got your tongue?"

Matt's face split in a grin. He shook his head, his teeth flashing white against his dark skin. "No, Casey Adams, I'm just not used to conducting business conversations across twelve feet of empty kitchen floor." He pushed away from the counter, the infuriating grin still in place. "Let's go somewhere where we can be more comfortable."

Alarm bells went off in Casey's head. "I'm quite comfortable in the kitchen, Mr. Stoner. It's where I make my living."

"Well, I don't, Mrs. Adams," Matt said, a hint of steel appearing in his tone. "I'm used to an office where there's a degree of comfort." He turned and walked toward the door. "Come on, we have a lot to discuss."

Ever the all-powerful business tycoon, Casey thought wrathfully. Rich men were all alike. But that small voice seemed to be laughing at her. "Are they?" it asked. "What other man in the world is like Matt Stoner—rich *or* poor?"

Shrugging off the voice, Casey grudgingly followed him to the study. She entered the room reluctantly. For a moment she was tempted to turn and run. There was a fire in the hearth and the lamps were turned low, casting amber pools of light on the green and burgundy of the carpet. Firelight flickered on the ivory paneling, creating shadows that moved mysteriously in the dim room. There was something sensuously disturbing about this room, with its dark-green velvet couch and the trace of wood smoke in the air. The very shadows seemed to hint at secret, stolen impulses.

Casey told herself she was being fanciful. She was tired, and that promoted silly thoughts. Matt Stoner was only a man.

She wandered toward the couch as Matt poured sherry into two glasses. Sinking onto the couch, she fixed her eyes on the flames that leaped in the fireplace as she rubbed her hands together nervously.

"Cold?"

Startled, Casey looked up. She hadn't heard him approach, but he was standing near her, holding the crystal glasses.

"No, why should I be?" she countered. "It's quite warm in here with the fire going."

"You were rubbing your hands together. I thought perhaps you were cold. Maybe you're just nervous."

"I have no reason to be nervous. Now maybe you'll get down to business. It *is* rather late."

He handed her the glass of sherry and settled onto the chair by the fireplace, glancing at the elegant watch that circled his brawny wrist. "It's not even midnight, Mrs. Adams. That's hardly late—unless, of course, you're Cinderella." He studied her with amused eyes. "You're not worried about pumpkins, are you?"

She shook her head. "No pumpkins, Mr. Stoner," she murmured huskily, then tried to lighten the mood in the dim room. It was too intimate this way, with the fire crackling and the lights down low and Matt Stoner sitting across from her, sipping his sherry, his eyes turning that smoky gray she had come to love already. She glanced down at the loafers she wore on her feet and smiled wryly. "Not even glass slippers."

Matt's eyes lazily traveled the length of her body, and the effect she had tried so gamely to chase away was back again with full force. She began to tremble, as if there were a motor running somewhere deep inside her, vibrating throughout her body. She was throbbingly aware of her breasts thrusting against her lace-covered bra. She could feel the nipples rising and tightening, and an almost painful ache engulfed her. Briefly she closed her eyes against the new knowledge that shattered her: She wanted Matt Stoner. Dear God, how she wanted him.

"You're not sleeping, are you, Mrs. Adams?"

Her eyes flew open. Could he tell what she had been thinking? Could he see through the sheer silk of her blouse that her nipples were taut with desire and straining against the fragile lace of her bra, as if frantic for his touch? Heated blood rushed into her face.

"No, I'm not sleeping."

The quiet in the room was almost a physical torment. She wanted to get up and run away. Or did she? Perhaps she really wanted to stay, to lie back on this velvet couch and drift away on a cloud of sensual pleasure.

Frightened by her thoughts, Casey gulped at her sherry,

then sputtered when the fiery liquid burned her throat.

"Not so fast, Casey Adams," Matt said. "That's potent stuff." A lazy smile warmed his features, sending cascades of pleasure over her.

Why did everything he say have to have a double meaning? Surely he was just mouthing innocuous social conversation. Then why did the word *potent* linger in her mind, conjuring up visions of muscular, hair-roughened limbs entwined with hers?

Aghast at that image, Casey stood up abruptly and began to pace the room. "The sherry's very nice, Mr. Stoner—"

"Matt."

"Matt." She took a breath to steady herself and continued. "But it's getting late and we've not even begun to discuss this business you said you wanted to talk about."

"Why did you wear blue jeans tonight, Casey?" he asked suddenly.

Startled by his question, she whirled around to face him. Hadn't he been listening to a thing she said? Lord, what a willful man!

"I beg your pardon?"

"I asked why you wore blue jeans. Do you always cook in that get-up?"

"Sometimes." She shrugged. "I'm comfortable in jeans. I don't have to worry about getting dirty."

"I thought that was why they invented the apron."

"I suppose it is," she said, smiling. "Come to think of it."

Matt rested his head against the back of his chair and regarded her with speculative eyes. "I do believe you could look sexy in a paper bag, Casey Adams. You're the first woman in jeans who's turned me on since I was a teenager."

"Turned . . . turned you on?" She could only stare helplessly at the door beyond her nemesis. *Now* what could she say? This was all going too fast for her. What if he got up and tried to seduce her? Her body trembled again at that thought. Oh dear God, yes, she prayed, please let him seduce me. . . .

"That's right," Matt said smoothly, "but let's get down

to that business we were going to talk about."

Of all the infuriating, maddening things to say! She wanted to talk about *them* now, not about business. Couldn't he see that? Was he blind? Totally feebleminded? Suppressing the desire to snap at him through gritted teeth, Casey once again sat down on the couch. At least she could say one thing for herself—she wasn't going to let him know that she was dying for him to kiss her. She could be as cool and unruffled as this vexing man who sat opposite her.

Taking a sip of her sherry, she met his eyes with her own cool, green ones. "Do go on, Mr. Stoner."

"Matt."

She took a measured breath to calm down. "Matt," she said with teeth-gritting precision. "I feel as though I've been waiting for you to come to the point for hours."

"The point is this, Casey. I want to hire you for the month of May."

Baffled, she stared at him. "You want to hire me," she repeated. "For the month of May?" She shook her head. "I'm afraid I don't understand."

"I want you to work for me, exclusively."

"But that's absurd! I own a business. I don't just hire myself out to the highest bidder. I run a *business*, Mr. Stoner."

"Matt."

She shot up from the couch. "Oh, for God's sake, will you *stop* that?"

"Call me Matt and I will," he said amiably.

"You are the most infuriating man I have ever met, Mr. Stoner."

"Matt."

She closed her eyes and tried counting to ten. It did no good. She opened them and saw him grinning at her.

"All right," she said tiredly. "Matt." She tried another tack. "You see, Matt," she said sweetly, suppressing the desire to strike that complacent expression off his arrogant face, "it's like this. I'm a businesswoman. I own my own business and I run it. It's very rare for me to do the cooking now. I hire others for that. I'm too busy planning the menus and supervising and administering. Tonight was just a fluke. I'd be willing to let you hire one of my chefs, but I'm not for sale."

He shook his head decisively. "Uh uh," he growled. "I want you."

For a moment she was tempted to think he meant those words in another context, but she shook herself mentally and started pacing again. "It's just not possible. Tonight was an exception."

"Why was tonight an exception?"

"Because it was a challenge. I wanted to prove to Stefanos Christopoulis that Boston cooking was as good as any other." A satisfied smile crossed her face. "And I did, too."

"Yes, you did, and that's why I need you, Casey. Tonight, just before he left, Stefanos agreed to come to my summer home on Cape Cod for extended talks. We'll be going there in late April and will stay until Memorial Day weekend. And I want you there, too. You're my ace in the hole, Casey. That man's the fussiest eater I've ever met. He carries a suitcase filled with antacids. You'd think he was a traveling pharmacy."

Anger rippled under Casey's placid surface. His ace in the hole, was she? All her original suspicions of him were confirmed. He was like every other wealthy man she had ever met—he used people for his own purposes, then discarded them.

She shook her head coolly. "No. And that's final."

Matt tilted his head to one side, studying her. "It wouldn't be all work, Casey."

A curious flutter attacked her midsection, elbowing her anger aside. She regarded him cautiously, then nonchalantly picked up her glass. "Oh? Why not?"

"You'd only have to plan the menus and supervise their preparation, and maybe cook an occasional meal that was very special. I'll bring Mary O'Reilly with me, and she can do most of the cooking. Other than that, you'd be free to relax and come and go as you wish. Sort of like an extended vacation. I've done some checking, Casey, and I hear you haven't taken a vacation in five years."

Casey ran her finger around the rim of her glass. It sounded inviting. She loved the Cape, and she was getting tired of the daily grind. It had been five long years of hard work and little play.

But who would run the business while she was away? The answer popped into her head almost immediately. Joanie. Joanie, who was turning out to be a top-notch assistant and who needed a chance to try her wings alone.

"It's impossible," she said out loud, shaking her head firmly and closing her mind to the insistent voice that urged her to accept. "A month," the voice said. "A month of lolling around on the beach, of sun and sea air and running across dunes. A month of being with Matt Stoner. . . ."

"No!" The word was uttered with unnecessary force, as if to ward off the last thought that had entered her head. "I mean, it's preposterous. Unthinkable, really. I just couldn't." Her eyes fluttered uneasily toward Matt, and she was annoyed by the amiable expression on his face. "And don't pester me about it," she snapped. "The subject's closed."

"Methinks the lady doth protest too much," he said softly.

"And don't quote Shakespeare at me!"

Matt's grin widened. "You're awfully pretty when you're angry, Casey Adams. Has anyone ever told you that?"

As a matter of fact, someone had. Andy had been fond of saying that, teasing her out of her tempers, telling her that her Irish blood needed thinning.

Casey studied Matt Stoner, contrasting him to her deceased husband. They were very different men. Andy had been tall and wiry, with a mop of blond hair that had constantly fallen into his eyes. He had been her high school sweetheart and not much more than a young man when he died. In her mind he would remain a boy forever. She couldn't even imagine what he would have matured to be. Certainly not like this solid man who sat before her. Matt was all hard lines and strong muscles, carved out of sinew and bones, with harsh planes in his brooding face and a square jaw that looked like granite. He was completely, inexorably male. And he was here, alive, sitting across from her, within range of a touch. Andy was gone, had been gone for five years. Was she to spend the rest of her life with only memories for comfort, or would she be able to reach out at last and try to find another love, someone warm and strong who could fill her life with light again?

Once again Casey realized she was vibrantly aware of her body and its reactions to Matt. Trembling slightly, she sat on the edge of the couch. Her hands were clasped tightly in front of her, and she leaned forward as though to catch the warming rays of the fire. Except she didn't need that warmth. There was enough inside her, spreading through her veins with intensifying heat, radiating from the engine that raced in her heart outward to her limbs, swelling into a crescendo of physical need.

She sat in what seemed like suspended animation, listening to the distant ticking of a grandfather clock, hearing the sudden spray of cinders and sparks as a log fell in the grate, seeing nothing but the blur of colors in the oriental rug at her feet, all the while painfully aware of Matt Stoner's presence just a few feet away.

His low, insistent voice throbbed with a sensual quality. "Come to the Cape with me, Casey."

A shiver feathered across her skin. She could feel her nipples growing taut, thrusting sensuously against the lace of her bra, throbbing with a desire that matched the insistent pulsing in her veins. She resolutely continued to stare into the fire.

The room was just too quiet. Surely he could hear her breathing, would know that it had slowed to a lazy sensuality. And perhaps he could see what was unguarded in her eyes, could tell that her body had softened for him, had grown warm, was pulsing with readiness.

Five years! she thought. Five years since she'd felt like this. Five years of dreaming about it, of tortured nights remembering it, of searching for it, and suddenly, here, in this dim, firelit room, she'd found it. . . .

"Casey."

She looked up to find him standing over her. Dear God,

why did he have to be so attractive? How could she fight him when all her senses were clamoring for him to hold her and kiss her, to make love to her?

"Casey, are you coming to the Cape with me or do I have to try a little friendly persuasion?"

"Friendly persuasion?" She swallowed with difficulty. "I don't know what you mean."

"I think you do."

"No, really." She shook her head and tried to sound convincing, and knew that he saw right through her.

But then he was beside her on the couch, and there was no more need for pretense. She felt his thumb brush across her cheek, felt his fingers fasten firmly on her chin and turn her face to his. She watched, fascinated, as his lips approached hers.

"Come to the Cape with me," he whispered.

Her lips parted to protest, but the words were trapped when his mouth brushed softly yet insistently against hers. When he lifted his mouth, she tried to steel herself against him.

"No," she whispered.

His lips came back, firmer this time, opening slightly as if to taste her, then left. "Say yes," he breathed.

Somewhere in the back of her mind it struck her that if she continued to refuse, he would continue to kiss her. She groaned softly. "No."

But he wasn't paying attention. His lips were tracing the sensitive pathways of her neck, nibbling the soft, creamy skin that seemed to vibrate under his touch, moving sensuously over her cheek toward her lips and brushing insistently back and forth, each kiss growing more tantalizing.

"Say yes, Casey."

But how could she say anything when his mouth was covering hers, when his lips were parting hers and his tongue was beginning a slow, voluptuous exploration of her mouth? His tongue was like fire, warming her, playing with her, probing and circling and making love to her, unhurriedly, deliberately seducing her into abandon.

She tried to push him away but he outmanuevered her,

encircling her with his arms, inexorably pressing her backward until her head was cushioned on the plump pillows
and her body was pinned beneath his. Her breath caught in
her throat and flames leaped in her veins. Gasping, she
fought to free her lips, her hands flat against the granite
wall of his chest.

"Matt, please . . ."

It made no difference. His lips were nibbling on her ear
lobe, then, in a sudden onslaught, his tongue flicked into
her ear, sending shuddering spasms of desire through her.
From far away she heard a low groan and realized it had
come from her, but then everything went black as she was
pulled into the vortex of her desire.

Hungrily she turned her mouth to his, straining to find
his lips. Her hips arched against that hard male contour that
pressed her to the couch. Frantically she clutched at his
shoulders, digging her fingers into the sinewed strength of
his back, all the while desperately aware of the ancient,
instinctive rhythm that was rocking their bodies.

When Matt moaned her name, Casey steeled herself,
suddenly aware of exactly who was holding her, caressing
her, loving her. She forced herself to lie still beneath him,
then felt a rush of cool air as Matt levered himself away
from her, rising up on his elbows to stare down at her with
stormy gray eyes.

"By God, woman," he grated, "you'll come to the Cape
with me or I'll take you right here."

Pushing away from him, Casey sat up on the couch, her
body still trembling with desire. Why was she fighting it?
Didn't she know by now that her body was truer to her than
her mind? It had known all along something she hadn't dared
admit to herself: She wanted Matt Stoner. She didn't know
him, didn't understand him, wasn't even sure she liked him,
but she wanted him.

"Yes," she said, her voice wavering unsteadily. "I think
perhaps I will go with you."

"Yes," he murmured lazily, his hand moving under her
tunic to unclasp her bra. "I think perhaps you will. . . ."

The sound of her bra being unhooked was a soft explosion

that reverberated in the air; the rustle of silky and lacy
materials moving over her sensitized skin was magnified a
thousand times. Nothing else existed. The other sounds of
the room—the crackling of the fire, the ticking of the clock—
all were gone now, dwarfed by these other, more intimate,
rustlings. Everything about her was acutely attuned to physical sensations—to Matt's calloused palm cupping the ripe
curve of her breast, to the teasing scrape of his thumbnail
against the hard nub of her nipple, to the harsh, almost
painful intake of her breath as a bolt of sensual pleasure
zagged through her, triggering intense desire. Everything
seemed to be in slow motion. How strange it all was! Hungry
for him, she had expected hot, urgent kisses, frantic thrust-
ings, fingers digging achingly into corded muscles. Instead,
her body seemed to be melting, languishing sensuously under the expert guidance of Matt's knowing touch. Her lips
parted as her head bent back to allow his mouth to explore
at his leisure. She reveled in his stimulating touch, throatily
laughing and moaning simultaneously. Her body once again
moved sinuously, her hips arching provactively, her breasts
thrust out to receive the quick, hot lashes from Matt's tongue.

"Ohhhh," she groaned. "Ohh, yesss . . ."

Matt shifted his body to unzip her jeans, and Casey lifted
her hips in a daze as he slid the pants down the long length
of her legs. Her lacy bikini panties followed, so that she
lay naked on the soft velvet couch. She raised her heavy
eyelids and met the stormy gaze above her. It shattered her,
sending hot waves of passion rippling through her. Her green
eyes widened and she caught her breath as Matt stood and
removed his shirt. Her breasts ached for the feel of that
hair-roughened chest, but she closed her eyes as he continued to undress, barely able to contain the rapturous need
that was building in her.

And then the warmth of his skin was burning hers, all
hard, male flesh, all corded muscles and granitelike tendons.
She gasped at the pleasure, her ears once again filled with
a rushing sound as his hands slid over her body. She felt
his tongue on her nipples, heard the tiny, wet sucking sounds
and thought she would go mad with desire. Her fingers

moved into his thick hair, forcing his head to remain at her breasts.

As if he would move, she thought! His lips and tongue seemed tireless, nibbling, tasting, sucking on her, driving her to a frenzy. But then he was moving despite her, and she found no need to guide his head. He knew where to lick, where to kiss her, where to let his teeth nip gently, where to brush his lips or nuzzle his nose into the soft ivory of her skin.

"Matt," she moaned. "Ohhhh, yessss..."

What was he *doing* to her? How did his lips and teeth and tongue find such intimate places to probe? What was happening to her? She was opening, flowering, yielding, all softness and mewing pleasure. And he—all hardness, everything she wasn't, finding her center, nuzzling, thrusting. Inside!

"Oh!" The cry escaped her, shouted into the dim room. "Oh, yes!" Moving, moving. Firm, hard, soft, yielding. Thrusting.

"Yes!"

8

CASEY STRETCHED LUXURIOUSLY, feeling the delicious tug of well-exercised muscles. Yawning sleepily, she tried to turn over onto her back, but a warm wall of flesh blocked her way. Momentarily disoriented, she lay with her eyes closed and listened to the morning sounds. When she didn't hear the peaceful ticking of her clock, she frowned slightly, then her eyes flew open.

Sunlight was sifting through matchstick bamboo blinds into a strange bedroom, to lie on a deep-blue carpet in a myriad pattern of horizontal lines. It all came back to her then, with stunning clarity. She was in Matt Stoner's bedroom, in the massive bed to which he had carried her sometime past midnight. Smiling dreamily, she raised her arms over her head and stretched again, then turned her head and met Matt's lazy gray eyes.

"I'm glad you're the kind of woman who's in a good mood in the morning," he muttered, his lips already nuzzling the rising peak of her breast. "I like my women happy."

A low, satisfied laugh escaped her. "No problem there, sir. You make your women *very* happy." Her hands moved up his broad back, over the rippling bands of muscles, to bury themselves in the rich, black thickness of his hair. "Mmmmmm," she murmured softly. "That feels good."

His tongue circled the pink aureole of her left breast and then slid downward, flicking fire at her navel and stopping to examine her hipbone. He was doing it again, she thought, her mind beginning to whirl unsteadily. He was weaving that magic, casting that spell that made her go absolutely mad with desire. What was it about his touch that ignited such fires in her?

Moaning, Casey arched her hips as Matt's lips slid lower. Transported to dizzying heights of passion, she clutched at his head, her heartbeat hammering against the soft wall of her breast. But she came back to earth with a thud when Matt raised his head and grinned devilishly at her.

"No breakfast for me this morning," he said. "I'm on a diet."

She stared at him for a moment, then reached for a pillow and threw it at him. "You beast! How dare you!"

"How dare I what?" he asked roguishly. "How dare I start your motor and then leave it idling?"

She angrily threw her legs over the side of the bed and sat up. "That's one way, the coarse way, of putting it," she snapped.

"Why be so offended, Casey? You told me I was coarse the first time you met me. Or was it the second time?"

She tugged a blanket loose and wrapped it around her. "If it wasn't the first time, it should have been," she said, then her mouth relaxed into a smile. "You really are a beast, you know."

One hand snaked under the blanket and cupped her breast. "I know. And you love it."

With a swift intake of breath, she lay back on the pillows. "I don't," she whispered, closing her eyes against the heady sensations that were shaking her as he stroked her breast, his thumb coaxing her nipple to taut arousal.

"You do." His breath was warm against her skin. "Say you do, Casey," he demanded softly. "Admit it."

Against her will, her arms left the warmth of the blanket and crept around Matt. "Well," she murmured huskily. "Perhaps just a little. . . ."

An hour later she lay in bed and watched Matt dress. He stood bare-chested, zipping his fly, then buckling the expensive leather belt that circled his trim waist.

"Where's your house on the Cape?" she asked, folding her arms under her head so she could see him better.

"Woods Hole," he answered. "Overlooking the harbor."

"What's it like?" she continued, not really caring what he answered, her eyes feasting on his broad, solid chest.

An odd twinkle entered his gray eyes. "Oh, it's just a regular summer cottage. Nothing spectacular."

She smiled in answer, feeling gloriously happy. "Will there be room for Stefanos and me and everyone else who'll have to be there?"

Matt seemed to deliberate, then flung her a grin. "Just barely, but you won't mind being cozy, will you?"

Her smile broadened. "I guess I can stand it."

Shrugging into a shirt, Matt approached the bed and leaned down to kiss her. "You're very pretty in the morning, Casey Adams. How come you've stayed unmarried all these years?"

She reached up and slid her hands into the cloud of hair that covered his chest. "Just ornery, I guess."

Grinning, he nudged his hip against hers. "Give me some room, woman. I feel the urge to get closer."

"Oh no you don't. You told me you have an important meeting at ten. And anyway I have to get home." She sat up and pushed her hair away from her face. "Do business tycoons always have important meetings on Sunday mornings at ten?" she asked.

"Not always, but this morning Stefanos wants to meet with me to settle a few last-minute details before he goes back to Greece. Pam is with him now, so I'd better get going."

A shadow seemed to cross the sun. Casey pushed away from the pillows. "Speaking of Miss Tyrone, how did she get home last night?"

Matt stood to finish dressing. "She went with Stefanos and Anna Copeland. She escorted them back to their hotel and stayed in a room near theirs, in case they needed anything."

In spite of herself, Casey felt her eyebrow rising. "She's quite the efficient secretary, isn't she?"

Matt smoothed the collar of his shirt and began tying his tie. "Best one I've ever had."

"Efficient *and* beautiful." Casey gave an exaggerated sigh. "Some men have all the luck."

"Do I detect a note of jealousy?"

"Why should I be jealous? *I* spent the night with you, didn't I?"

"So you did, and if you're not careful, you'll be spending every night with me. You could get to be a habit, woman."

Euphoria soared inside Casey. She felt marvelously happy. Everything seemed complete with Matt Stoner. He made delicious love to her, he made her laugh, and he was intelligent, one of the few men who stretched her mind and challenged her intellect. And, Pam Tyrone wasn't his mistress.

Clasping her hands around her legs, she rested her chin on her knees. "I don't know why you say that," she said innocently. "Last night wasn't all that special for me...."

With a muffled curse, Matt crossed the room with lightning speed and gathered her into his arms, stinging her neck with passionate kisses that sent her into spasms of laughter.

"You lie," he growled. "Repent, woman! Repent or I'll ravish you right here."

"Repent?" she laughed. "You think I'd do a fool thing like that with the threat of ravishment hanging over my head?"

He sat back and grinned at her, and there was a moment of perfect happiness. Casey felt it and knew Matt felt it, too. It was one of those rare times when everything is right and perfection exists for a few seconds. Reaching up, she smoothed her hand through his rumpled hair. "I repent," she whispered, feeling a strange sense of contentment. She didn't understand it and didn't want to analyze it, but something wonderful had happened when she met Matt Stoner, something that had triggered a landslide of happiness in her life.

Matt leaned down and kissed her once lingeringly, then gave her another, more perfunctory, kiss before standing. "I've got to go. I'll call you, Casey."

He threw her a wave from the door, and she lay back against the pillows, listening to his footsteps retreating down the hall. Sighing, she sat up and threw her legs over the edge of the bed. After insisting that she not drive here last night, that he would bring her home after dinner, here she was, left behind to call a taxi or walk.

Men, she thought wryly. Of all the exasperating, infuriating, wonderful creatures on earth.

On Monday morning Joanie Simpson stood in front of Casey's desk and stared into her employer's dream-drugged eyes.

"Well, you look mighty happy this morning. What gives? You win the lottery or something?"

Casey pulled herself out of her daydreams and smiled lazily. "Or something."

"What's that supposed to mean?"

Casey swiveled her chair to face the window. "Nothing. Everything." Grinning, she looked back at Joanie. "I've gone a little crazy, I guess." She glanced at her calendar. "It's April first."

"What's so great about April first?"

Casey sighed and leaned on her elbow. "Spring's almost

here, Joanie. And I've decided to take a vacation."

"A vacation? You? By God, you *have* gone crazy!"

"Well, it's a kind of working vacation," Casey said, laughing.

"A working vacation," Joanie repeated, then drew up a chair. "Okay, tell me everything. I'm all ears."

"Matt Stoner has asked me to go to the Cape with him at the end of the month. Stefanos Christopoulis will be there for business talks, and Matt wants me to do the cooking—or at least supervise it and plan the meals."

Joanie's eyebrow rose. "Oh, so now it's Matt, not Mr. Stoner. What happened when he took you home? Did you two get chummy?"

A shutter came down over Casey's face. Though she valued Joanie as a colleague and friend, she wasn't about to share what had happened between Matt and her. "You know I always end up calling my clients by their first names. Why should it be different with Matthew Stoner?"

"Because he's Matthew Stoner and notorious with the ladies, that's why," Joanie said. "And I distinctly remember your saying last week that he wasn't your type. And anyway, I saw the look on your face when I came in. You looked like a cat who's just lapped up a bowlful of cream. So what gives?"

Casey picked up her glasses and set them firmly on her nose. "Absolutely nothing. And instead of wondering what gives with me and Matthew Stoner, you'd better start concentrating on learning all the little details that I usually cover. I'm leaving you in charge of the business for the whole time I'm gone. Think you can handle it?"

Joanie's face paled. "Me? In charge?" She sat looking into space, all interest in Casey and Matt Stoner apparently gone.

By mid-afternoon Casey had finished up her work and was ready to meet with one of her clients, Dorothea Fensterwick, at a local hotel. Casey frowned slightly at what lay ahead of her. Dorothea had never been an easy client. The daughter of a wealthy Boston family, she had grown

accustomed to getting her own way in most matters. This
included the way she wanted parties to be held. This year
she had decided on a lavish formal dance at a hotel. Her
daughter was graduating from school in May, and Dorothea
had decided to give her a party that everyone would remember for years. It was up to Casey to make everything
memorable—and to make sure it all went off without a
hitch. While Casey had no doubts she could do so, she did
have doubts about her ability to deal with Dorothea. More
than once they had tangled over party details, and each time
it had gotten progressively more difficult for Casey to smile
and nod acquiescence. This time, if Dorothea interfered,
Casey wasn't sure she would be able to rein in her temper.
Perhaps the time had come to lay down the law according
to Casey Adams to Dorothea.

Casey walked through the Common and the Public Garden, and by the time she arrived at the hotel she knew her
cheeks were rosy from the brisk air. Her thick hair bounced
on her shoulders as she walked into the lobby, her stride
fresh with anticipation. Not even the thought of meeting
Dorothea could dampen the enthusiasm that had engulfed
her as she walked. It was a beautiful day. How could everyone be so wrong about April first? It wasn't April Fool's
Day, it was the most perfect day in the calendar year. Of
course, the fact that she had made mad love with Matt Stoner
might account for this newfound fondness for the first day
of April.

Taking a seat in the dimly lit cocktail lounge, Casey
ordered club soda with a twist of lemon and then sat back
to wait for Dorothea Fensterwick to show up. She had been
there only a few moments when a silvery laugh drifted
toward her from the entrance to the bar.

Smiling, Casey listened absently to the fresh laughter,
thinking it must be a young girl in love, for there was so
much youthful joy in the sound. But another laugh, a deeper,
masculine laugh, joined the light-hearted giggle, and Casey's smile faded. She knew that laugh. It was a man's laugh,
hinting at sexual experience and robust appetite.

A feeling of dread washed over Casey. No, it couldn't

be. Of course it couldn't. What did it matter that he hadn't called her today? It was only Monday afternoon. She had seen him yesterday morning. Casey felt the beginnings of ice forming around her heart. Yes, only yesterday morning, in his bed.

Not wanting to, but knowing she must, Casey turned to peer through the luxurious foliage of a rubber tree. For a moment she chouldn't find them, then the laughter rang out again and her eyes zeroed in on a young girl with blond hair cascading down her back, whose attention was riveted on a tall, dark-haired man. Matt Stoner.

Casey's face stiffened. Swiveling her head around, she gulped at her club soda and made a face. She had always made it a policy not to drink any alcoholic beverage while she was working, but she quickly decided the situation at hand called for a change in policy. She signaled the waiter and ordered Scotch on the rocks.

"Make it a double," she added, her heart hammering in her breast. Her fingernails began a rapid tattoo on the table top. Of all the reprehensible louts. He was with that girl again, that youngster he had been seducing in his office. What was her name? Jewel? Pearl? Ah, Crystal. Yes, Crystal.

Casey downed a huge swallow of the Scotch and grimaced. Why had she let Matt Stoner get past her defenses? Why hadn't she followed her instincts about him? It had been sheer idiocy to let herself be sucked into that human whirlpool. How he must be laughing at her, figuring her for a fool. And how easily she had succumbed, like putty in his expert hands.

Dashing back a gulp of the expensive Scotch, Casey felt its impact down to her toes. Shuddering, she closed her eyes and tried to get a grip on herself. What a day this was turning out to be! What had she been saying about April first a little while ago? It looked as if she was rapidly turning out to be the biggest April fool of all.

As if Fate was anxious to compound matters, Casey heard Dorothea Fensterwick's imperious voice ringing in the lobby. It was getting louder, coming this way.

Casey would have to get a grip on herself. She needed all the poise she could muster. Why did it have to be at a time when it seemed that every bit of poise had deserted her?

"Darling!" Dorothea Fensterwick swept into the bar, a mink coat floating out behind her, diamonds flashing on her elegant hands. "You're here! And on time, too!"

For a minute Casey thought Dorothea had spotted her and was speaking to her, but then she realized that Dorothea was talking to someone else. Curious, Casey turned her head and received the second shock of that afternoon.

Dorothea was embracing the young blond who had been hanging on Matt's arm. And Matt was standing by, a look of affectionate amusement on his dark features. Pure hatred rippled through Casey. How she would like to get her hands on him. . . .

Then she turned her attention back to Dorothea and Crystal, and a niggling suspicion crept into her mind. No. It couldn't be. That would be too much. Casey cocked her head to one side and studied the two women, one tall and gray-haired with elegant clothes and a patrician face, the other tall and blond in the latest fashions, and with the spoiled, petulant manner of the ultrarich. Yes, there was a definite resemblance. In fact, there was a very strong resemblance, not only in their looks, but in the arrogant way they both acted.

Heaving a sigh, Casey took another sip of her Scotch. It looked as if she was going to need all the sustenance she could get, for she had the sneaking suspicion that Dorothea Fensterwick's daughter must be Crystal, the very same Crystal that Matt Stoner had been seducing in his office only a couple of weeks ago.

Looking up, Casey had her worst suspicions confirmed. Only things were even worse than she had thought, for tagging along behind the two women was Matt Stoner, an expression on his face at once unreadable and highly amused. Raising an ironic eyebrow, Casey acknowledged his presence and then promptly decided to ignore him altogether. She was darned if she would give him the time of day. But she was also darned if she would give him the satisfaction of appearing upset. Not on her life, she wouldn't. On *his* life, maybe—for she felt murderous rage at him—but that could be taken care of later, at a more propitious time. Right now she had to smile and act coolly professional.

Casey allowed a degree of warmth to enter her green eyes as she smiled up at the two women when they reached her table. "Dorothea, you're looking lovely."

"As you are, darling," Dorothea intoned. "But I have an excuse. I've just been in Paris for two weeks. What's yours? Where do you get that fabulous *color*, Casey? Surely not out of a jar!"

Casey's smile deepened. "It comes from walking briskly through the Common. I recommend it highly." She turned her head to look at Crystal. "And you must be Dorothea's daughter."

Crystal tossed her head, her blond curls dancing. "That's right. And you're Càsey Adams." She cast a coquettish look back at Matt. "I do believe we had another encounter recently, didn't we? At Matt's office?"

Casey felt her smile turn to vinegar. "That's right, I believe we did. But we won't mention that to your mother, will we?" she asked sweetly and was rewarded with a momentary look of fear in Crystal's eyes.

Dorothea glanced from one to the other. "What's this? You've met before? And what happened at Matt's office?" She put an imperious hand on Matt's arm, dragging him closer. "You've met Matt Stoner then, the man my daugher has set her cap for. Boston's biggest catch."

Casey smiled thoughtfully. "Oh, I don't know about that, Dorothea. I've seen swordfish bigger."

One thing Casey could say for Matt, he had a sense of humor. It came alive in his eyes, roguishly laughing at her. The same couldn't be said of Crystal or Dorothea, who stood by looking blank.

"What's that, Casey?" Dorothea asked. "Swordfish, you say?" She shook her head as if to clear out cobwebs and sat down with a flourish. "Oh well, I've never really understood you young career women," she said dismissingly.

Casey hid her smile behind a hand, but the laughter lurked in her green eyes. "We're a breed apart, Dorothea. We actually *like* making jokes." Flicking an acid look at Matt, she took out her notebook. "Now, perhaps we'd better get down to business. You said you wanted to invite two hundred to this dance?"

"At least," Crystal answered for her mother. "I'm even toying with the idea of five hundred." She tossed her golden hair and postured prettily. "I want a *real* splash!"

Casey's eyebrow lifted. "The more the merrier."

"Oh, Crystal," Dorothea sputtered. "Be reasonable! Five hundred guests! We don't know that many respectable people!"

It was Matt's turn to hide a smile behind a large hand. Seeing him, Casey couldn't help but grin in response. How ironic it all was—here Dorothea was talking about not knowing enough respectable people, and the most disreputable man in Boston was sitting right next to her!

"Well, I'll have to know the number of guests fairly soon," Casey said, trying to get back on track. "And what will you want to do about food? A light buffet at midnight, perhaps?"

"You're kidding!" Crystal scoffed. "I want a full six-course dinner, maybe eight, complete with champagne and caviar!"

Casey bit delicately at her lip, waiting for Dorothea to stop spluttering. "Crystal! You're such a spoiled child! Do you know what that would *cost*? We're not *made* of money, you know."

"You just spent enough in Paris on clothes to feed all of Latin America for a month," Crystal said hotly. "If you can do it, I can." A spoiled smile came over her face. "Daddy said so."

Casey rested her chin on her fist and looked from one to the other. A tug of war seemed to be raging between mother and daughter.

"You've spoken to your father about this?" Dorothea flared. "Behind my back?"

"It wasn't behind your back, Mother! You were in Paris,

remember? Buying new spring frocks?"

Mottled color crept into Dorothea's face. "I think we'd better discuss this at some other time, Crystal."

"Why?" she shot back defiantly. "I want to discuss it now. Mrs. Adams is here now and so is Matt." She turned her young face toward him, beaming. "Don't you think we should discuss it now, Matt darling?"

Casey could barely stop rolling her eyes. She settled for a discreet cough. "Perhaps your mother is right, Crystal. I can hardly be helpful if you two haven't decided on what you want."

"But *I've* decided!" Crystal sneered. "And I *always* get what I want." Her eyes slid provocatively toward Matt. "And *you'd* better pay attention, *Mr.* Stoner."

At this point Matt finally spoke up. "Crystal, I have to agree with Mrs. Adams. Why don't you and your mother and father thrash all this out after dinner tonight. What you're talking about is a little outlandish. A six-course dinner for five hundred people would cost all outdoors." He looked at Casey wryly. "Of course, Mrs. Adams wouldn't mind. She could retire to the south of France on the profits."

Crystal sat up sharply. "Matt! I thought you'd side with me! How can you be so cruel?"

"I'm not being cruel, Crystal, I'm being reasonable. It's something you could try cultivating once in a while."

Casey watched him thoughtfully. Perhaps she had been wrong about Matt Stoner. He wasn't acting like a lecher right now. In fact, he sounded a little like a stern but loving father.

Tears dashed down Crystal's cheeks. "But you know I need you to side with me! You *know* I do!"

"Why is that, Crystal?" Matt asked gently.

"Because . . . because I *want* you to," she shot back, a pout marring her pretty face.

"Ah, Crystal, that's one of the hardest lessons we have to learn in life. We don't always get what we want." Matt's voice was soft and warm, but steel lay underneath it.

As if sensing that, Crystal stood up, scraping her hand

over her flushed cheeks. "I hate you, Matthew Stoner! I *hate* you!" she choked, and then ran from the lounge.

Dorothea sighed and gathered up her mink. "Ah well, a little drama." Making a moue, she smiled at Casey. "I'll call you when we get this thing straightened out, Casey dear." Matt helped her stand, then Dorothea glanced back at Casey. "Don't think too harshly of Crystal, will you, Casey? She's spoiled rotten, but that's Herman's and my fault. She was born late and we love her dearly, but I'm afraid Matt is right. He's been telling us that it's time for her to grow up and stop being a spoiled child." Dorothea smiled sadly. "I'm sorry we didn't listen earlier, Matthew. And I suppose it's up to Herman and me to get on with it."

Dorothea walked slowly across the carpeted floor, her figure no longer as flamboyant as it had been when she entered. Casey felt a pang as she watched her go. She had never liked Dorothea, but she felt an affection for her now. What was that old Indian saying? Never judge anyone unless you've walked in their moccasins for at least a day. Of course, in Dorothea's case, they weren't moccasins but Gucci pumps, yet the point was well taken.

Then she met Matt's eyes and all her anger flooded back to her. Picking up her drink, she gulped it down in one swallow.

"And what's that you were saying to Dorothea, Matt?" she asked sweetly. "Something about it being time for dear little Crystal to grow up?" An acid smile crossed her face. "It sure looks like you're volunteering to help her, doesn't it, Mr. Stoner?"

9

MATT SAT FORWARD, loosely clasping his large hands in front of him on the table. Casey's eyes were drawn to them, and to the hair that crept out from under his immaculate white cuffs. She felt a chill of remembrance at how those hands had stroked her, building fires in her veins that only he seemed able to extinguish.

"You're jealous, Casey," he said softly, his voice tinged with amusement.

"I'm not!"

He chuckled quietly. "Yes, you are."

"Of that little child? Be serious, Matt!"

"I am being serious, now I'd like you to be."

"Don't be so sure of yourself, Matt, it ill becomes you." Casey signaled the waiter and ordered another Scotch.

Matt glanced at his watch, his eyebrows rising. "Two drinks before dinner, Casey? That's really tossing them down."

"I don't see that it's any concern of yours, Mr. Stoner," Casey said coldly. "I believe I told you once that I'm a big girl and I can take care of myself."

"Not when you're drunk, Mrs. Adams."

Casey bristled at the laughter in his eyes. "I'm hardly going to get drunk on two lousy drinks. Stop being so concerned," she said, adding sarcastically, "save it for Crystal."

"You *are* jealous!" he said triumphantly, slapping one large hand on the table.

Casey rolled her eyes and managed to look bored. "Believe it if you must, sir, but I haven't a jealous bone in my body."

"There's not a woman alive on the face of this earth who hasn't a jealous bone in her body," Matt said, his voice brooking no dispute.

Casey's eyes flashed. "You're a chauvinist!" she exclaimed. "Oh, I can't stand it."

"It isn't chauvinistic to recognize the facts and lay the cards on the table, Casey."

She closed her eyes as if tired and shook her head wearily. "All right, have it your way. You're the kind who always does, anyway."

"Well, I'm glad you recognize that, Casey Adams, because I'm beginning to get the distinct urge to have my way with you."

Casey's eyes flew open. "You're *what?*" she squeaked, trying to keep her voice low, although she was shaking with anger.

"You heard me. You're awfully pretty and I keep remembering what you look like without clothes on." He grinned at her. "And there're probably a few empty rooms upstairs with great big comfortable beds in them. How about it, Casey? You game for a romp in the hay before dinner?"

"You . . . you cad," she breathed. "How dare you talk

like that when you've just probably come from one of those great big comfortable beds with sweet little honey-pie Crystal Fensterwick!"

—Matt's grin widened, if that were possible. "What were you saying about not being jealous, Mrs. Adams?"

"You see!" Casey swept on. "You don't even deny it! Oooooohhhh, you're such a lecher!"

"Casey, it's hardly lecherous to be with a beautiful woman and get the urge to make love to her. That's entirely normal. It's how we populate this great planet of ours. So how about it?"

"I'll bet you've done more than your share of populating this great planet of ours, Mr. Stoner," Casey said icily. "So you'll pardon me if I refuse to participate." Finishing her drink, she signaled for another.

"Three drinks, Casey?" he said solicitously.

"Three drinks, Matthew," she answered grimly.

"Is your name really Casey?" he asked suddenly.

"What else would it be? Matilda?"

He shook his head in amusement, his massive shoulders heaving gently with silent laughter. "I was wondering if it were short for something, that's all."

"No, my father named me after Casey Stengel, the baseball manager. Daddy used to say that Casey Stengel was the only person that made the Yankees human." Casey's eyes glittered with momentary humor. "Daddy was a great fan of the Red Sox, you know."

"Did he plan on your being a girl?"

"No, he wanted a boy. Had it all mapped out that his son would pitch for the Sox, then *I* was born." Casey smiled reminiscently. "I wish he could have known that I prepared a banquet for the Red Sox. He sure would have been proud."

"He's dead, then?"

Casey nodded. "Years ago. I was still in high school."

"And your mother?"

"She died soon after I married Andy."

"And then Andy died, too?"

Casey sat quietly, thinking back to that time five years

ago, then she nodded. "Yes," she said softly. "Then he died, too."

Matt sat silently, watching as she finished her third drink, then he stood up and looked down at her from what seemed to Casey to be a great height.

"You just stay here, Casey. I'll be back in a minute, you hear?"

She nodded slowly, feeling slightly dizzy. The Scotch had been strong, and she hadn't had time to eat more than a salad for lunch. Perhaps Matt had been right. She shouldn't have had so much to drink.

He was back before she knew it, sliding into the chair next to hers, his muscular shoulder bumping hers gently. "You feeling all right?" he asked softly.

She took a moment to answer. Actually, she wasn't feeling all that well. After starting out so perfectly well, the day had turned into a disaster. Tears threatened to swim into her eyes, but Casey blinked them away.

"I feel all right," she said, but knew she sounded oddly weak.

"You're a gutsy little lady, Casey Adams," Matt murmured.

This time the tears wouldn't be blinked away. They filled her eyes and threatened to overflow. What was the matter with her? Why did it affect her so much to hear that strange, gentle solicitude in Matt Stoner's voice? Maybe, a quiet voice answered, because there are so few people in your life who are gentle with you.

"Casey." Matt's voice was disturbingly close to her ear. So close that she could feel his breath warm on her cheek. And what was his arm doing around her shoulders? No matter, it felt good there. In fact, it felt *right* there, so she wasn't going to protest.

"Casey, I'm bringing you upstairs," Matt said.

She turned her head and felt alarmingly dizzy. "Upstairs? Whatever for?"

He looked so tender, so kind, that the tears started to overflow. "To put you to bed, that's what for."

The old alarm went off. "You cad," she said, slurring her speech slightly. "Here I am threatening to be sick and all you can think of is bed."

Matt was grinning at her. "You sure think an awful lot of me, don't you?" he asked, then stood and swept her into his arms.

Startled, she could only cling to his massive shoulders and hope she didn't get seasick. "Are you really walking through this lobby, Matthew Stoner?" she asked, closing her eyes and burying her head in his shoulder.

"I sure am."

"Are there really people staring at us?"

"There sure are."

She heard elevator doors close behind them and ventured a sigh of relief. "Are we alone now?"

"Mmm hmmmm."

She opened her eyes and stared up into teasing gray ones. "You're a remarkable man, Matthew Stoner," she said.

"And you're a remarkable woman," he answered.

She put her head down on his shoulder and went to sleep.

"Do much drinking, Casey?" Matt asked conversationally.

Casey groaned and held an ice pack to her aching head. "Oh shut up."

Matt sipped his sherry. "I can recommend the hair of the dog that bit you."

She groaned again. "No Scotch. Never again."

"You only had three."

"Three doubles."

His eyebrows rose. "Ah, then that explains it a little better."

Putting down the ice pack, Casey pushed her hair back and squinted at the clock that sat on the bedside table. "What time is it?"

"Almost midnight."

"How long did I sleep?"

"Almost six hours."

"And why are *you* still here? I feel like the dying man who wakes up and sees vultures flying overhead."

Matt chuckled softly, shaking his head. "Always complimentary about me, aren't you, Casey?"

"You bring it on yourself. You're the one who keeps squiring young blonds around who are young enough to be your daughter."

"So we're back to Crystal again."

"So it appears."

"Will you let me explain about Crystal?"

"Go ahead. I could use a good laugh right about now."

Matt's good humor seemed to be rapidly disappearing. "Casey, shut up or I'll quiet you myself."

"Ever the robust he-man, aren't you, Matthew?"

Matt's eyes glittered warningly. "Casey, be careful."

Sighing, she waved a hand airily. "Oh, go ahead and explain."

"Herman and Dorothea Fensterwick are old friends of my family—"

"Hardly surprising," Casey commented, suppressing a yawn. "Money always knows money."

Obviously biting back a sharp retort, Matt continued evenly. "A couple of months ago I was at their home for dinner, and young Crystal was home from boarding school. I hadn't seen her for three or four years and commented on how pretty she was becoming. 'A regular young lady' were the words I used, I believe."

Casey raised an ironic brow, but refrained from comment.

"Well, she must have gotten the idea of trying out her newly found feminine wiles on me, because the next day she showed up at my office." A grin widened on Matt's face. "You should have seen what she was wearing—a slinky black dress with the buttons undone practically down to her navel and tottering on black high heels that looked like stilts." Matt chuckled in reminiscence, but Casey only breathed fire. "Anyway, she leaned over my desk to ask for a light and I saw down her dress halfway to Christmas."

"What a thrill," Casey said dryly.

Matt flicked her a glance, but went on. "I tried to be as tactful as possible—"

"Oh, I'll bet."

"But she wouldn't take a hint." Matt's eyes had grown steely as he threw Casey a warning glance. "Anyway, I realized she was young and impressionable, and would only find someone else to try out her wiles on, so I—"

"Volunteered," Casey said, shrugging elaborately. "Naturally."

Matt took a deep breath. "So I decided I'd play along with her, since some other man might take unfair advantage and she'd end up getting really hurt."

Casey held a hand to her cheek, gazing at Matt with wide, adoring eyes. "God, you're wonderful, Matt," she sighed, batting her eyelashes at him.

His face suddenly looked like a thundercloud. "And you, Casey Adams, are cruising for trouble."

"Just like Crystal!" she exclaimed, sitting up and flouncing her hair. "Will you take care of me, too, Mr. Stoner?"

She thought she had gone too far, but then saw amusement creeping into his gray eyes. He crossed his arms and stared at her thoughtfully. "Would you like to eat some dinner?"

"At midnight? Don't they close down the kitchens?"

"Do you think they'd refuse Matt Stoner?"

She rolled her eyes heavenward. "Would anyone?" she said, throwing her hands up as if the answer were clear.

"So what would you like for your midnight dinner?"

Casey eyed him speculatively. If she was with one of the wealthiest men in Boston, why not enjoy it?

"Filet mignon and fresh asparagus, if they have it, otherwise artichokes in lemon butter," she answered, ticking off each item on a slim finger. "A small salad also, please."

"And your wine, madam?"

"Something French and expensive," she said flippantly.

When Matt finished ordering, he turned back to Casey. "Anyway, the day you walked in on Crystal and me, I was giving her a lesson. Unfortunately, she didn't learn anything from it."

Casey nodded her head wisely. "Oh, she learned something, all right. You won't shake her now for all the tea in the harbor."

"Why do you say that, Casey? Because I'm so desirable?"

Casey realized the trap of her words too late. Seeing the teasing expression on his face, she sniffed expressively. "You've got to be kidding. *You,* desirable?"

"You seemed to think so Saturday night and Sunday morning," Matt said, walking slowly toward the bed where Casey sat.

She knew she should move, but was darned if she'd give him the satisfaction. "I didn't want to hurt your feelings, Matt. Men's egos are so fragile, you know."

His teeth flashed in a grin. And then Casey began to be really alarmed. She hadn't noticed before, but he had discarded his suit jacket and vest, and had unbuttoned the top buttons of his shirt. Damn the man, he didn't wear an undershirt. The hairs on his chest were a blatant statement of his virility. Casey's eyes wandered downward, and she saw he had rolled up his sleeves, exposing sun-toasted forearms, their sinewed paths furrowed by veins and sprinkled with soft hair. And he was sitting down on the edge of the bed. And that was way too close. . . .

She tried to bolt off the other side, but a hand snaked out and caught her wrist. Matt effortlessly pulled her backward and into his arms.

"You little hellion," he murmured against her throat. "Where did you think you'd run to?"

"The bathroom?" she asked weakly, all the while aware of his hands moving sensuously up and down her back, molding her body to his . . . of his lips traveling across her neck and down one shoulder, nipping as they went.

"Casey, why don't I cancel that room-service order?" Matt suggested, one hand pushing the collar of her blouse away in irritation.

"Absolutely not," she answered. "I'm famished."

"So am I." Matt's lips traveled down the vee of her blouse and into the shadowy valley between her breasts. "For you."

Casey was beginning to wonder why she was protesting. Delicious tremors were shaking her body as Matt's large hand deftly unfastened the row of pearl buttons that ran down her blouse. His teeth nipped playfully at her bra strap, then he pushed it aside and unfastened her bra, exposing the creamy, pink-tipped globes to his seeking mouth.

Now all thoughts of protest were gone. Casey dug her fingers into his hair, guiding his mouth to the aroused peaks of her breasts, moaning blissfully as his tongue began erotically licking them.

She tensed a moment later at a soft knock on the door. "Matt." She shook his shoulders slightly. "Matt, please stop."

He chuckled softly and continued licking the rosy crests. Frantically Casey realized she was caught in a treacherous dilemma—the ecstasy induced by Matt was warring with the terror of having a waiter walk in on them as they made love. Feebly Casey pounded on Matt's shoulders.

"Matt," she gasped, fighting a delicious spiral of desire that was spinning in her midsection. "Matt, the waiter . . ."

"Let him wait." Matt had transferred his attention to Casey's neck, nuzzling the pulse that fluttered wildly under the creamy translucence of her skin. His thumb brushed erotically back and forth across the nipple of her right breast, wreaking havoc with what little remained of her sensibilities.

She tried desperately to think, but found it almost impossible. His tongue was darting into her left ear, and his warm palm had covered her breast and was gently massaging it. In a final effort, she seized his hand and stopped the hypnotizing motion. "Matt." She took a deep breath to steady her erratic breathing. "Matt, the waiter is knocking at the door. We've got to stop."

"Like hell we do," he growled, and in one fluid movement ran his hand up her silken thighs toward the pulsating mound of her womanhood. Gasping, Casey sat up and somehow freed herself from his questing hand. Leaping off the bed, she raced for the bathroom and slammed the door behind her. Leaning back against it, her breathing ragged, her breasts heaving, she looked at herself in the bathroom mirror. Her blouse was unbuttoned and her bra unhooked. Her breasts were rosy-tipped, her cheeks blazing red, and her eyes flashing with green sparks of desire. Stunned, she could only stand and stare at herself. Who was this woman? Where had this vibrancy come from? For five long years Casey had been accustomed to the dull, empty ache of loveless nights. Her eyes sparkled only when she was angry, or perhaps when laughing with a few close friends. No man had been able to produce this euphoria, this pounding in the bloodstream, this incredible rush of physical desire. She felt alive, on fire with sensation. What was she doing hiding in the bathroom when the one man on earth who could make her feel like this was in the other room?

Taking a deep breath, she clutched the front of her blouse together and opened the door a crack.

"Matt?"

"Yes, Casey?" His low voice sounded amused. She bit at her lip and wondered why the room was so quiet. Had he let the waiter in? Was he even now setting out the dinner they had ordered? "Matt," she started, then hesitated. Screwing up her courage, she spoke more loudly. "Matt, send the waiter away. I . . . I'm not very hungry. . . ."

The door opened with a suddeness that sent her reeling backward. Grabbing at the sink, she stared into smoldering gray eyes as Matt advanced on her. Clutching her blouse closed, she darted a frightened glance behind Matt, toward the bedroom. "Matt," she whispered. "The waiter . . ."

By now Matt was within inches of her. He reached out and coaxed her blouse open, his hands covering her breasts as his mouth took hers. Swaying, Casey melted toward him, all thought of the waiter swept aside by the golden rush of desire that flooded through her. Twining her arms around his neck, she nestled further into his embrace, her breasts tingling at the feel of the wiry hairs that matted his chest.

"Matt," she whispered, her eyes closed in rapture. "Matt, make love to me."

He cupped the back of her head, his fingers digging into her cascading curls. "Ah, Casey Adams," he breathed. "I intend to. I intend to do just that."

Lifting her into his arms, he carried her back to the bed. She shivered in ecstacy as Matt slid her blouse off, then drew her bra away and began to loosen her skirt. Her nylons followed, stripped from her legs and tossed aside, floating out through the air like silk banners as Matt's hands went to the final barrier, the lace bikini panties.

"Why do women wear such provocative little things?" he whispered, letting his lips follow the course of her panties as he drew them down over her hips and the long expanse of legs.

She shuddered with pleasure, a smile quivering at her lips. "To drive men mad," she whispered throatily.

"You damn well succeed," he muttered, struggling with his belt buckle.

"Here. Let me help." She undid his belt, then lowered the zipper on his trousers. "Why do you men insist on wearing so many clothes?" she demanded, her eyes laughing provocatively into his.

He shucked off one leg of his trousers, then the other, and sent them sailing across the room, followed closely by his undershorts. "To drive you women crazy," he murmured, his eyes locked on hers.

She felt the electric shock of pleasure as his body moved onto hers. "Well you succeed," she whispered, wrapping her arms around the muscular body that held her captive. His hands roved at will, finding the warm, intimate places that gave her the most pleasure, his lips grazing her sensitized skin in hungry abandonment.

Pleasure cascaded over her. Her body arched, her hips lifting in readiness, her breasts rising to receive the bold thrust of his tongue. She grew faint from her desire. The room receded and the rushing started in her ears. She gasped, her lips parting as her hands dug into his back.

"Matt," she whispered. "Love me."

But he ignored her, concentrating instead on the pounding pulse in her neck, then transferring his attention to her ear lobe.

"Matt." She gripped his shoulders and tried to wriggle deeper underneath him. "Matt, please." Her heart pounded.

Her blood sizzled. "Matt. . . ."

He was so *slow!* He moved as if he were under water, his hands stroking her body, his lips traveling in lazy exploration, content to wander in a seemingly aimless fashion, and all the while she was on fire for him.

Her body moved in hypnotic, rhythmic fashion, her hips swaying provocatively. She was empty, so very empty, but also open and waiting, needing to be filled. She closed her eyes and hugged her arms around Matt's hard male body.

"Ohhh, please." She buried her head in the curve of his shoulder, clinging to him. *"Now."*

And then he answered her, his body filling her need, all hardness, all male strength, lowering to meet her as she rose, rising as she receded, rocking in time with her, in tune, as one.

"It's good," he breathed. "So good."

She opened her eyes and saw the shadowy beginnings of his beard, like a bruise on his jaw, and felt her heart lighten. Yes, she thought. So very, very good. . . .

And then there was no more thought. Only pleasure, searing, soaring, cascading pleasure, cresting in a furious frenzy, then falling off. Satisfied. . . .

It might have been hours later when Casey turned sleepily toward Matt and threw an arm across his chest. "Matt?" she asked drowsily.

"Mmmm?" He stroked her back, his hand moving lovingly from her shoulders to her waist and up again.

Shivering with delight, Casey moved closer, molding her body against his. "Matt, what ever happened to the waiter?"

"I sent him away," he murmured, his lips trailing across her shoulder.

"Before I asked you to?"

His grin flashed white in the dark room. "Yes, you little wanton, before you even asked me to."

Sighing softly, Casey closed her eyes, her cheek resting on the leanly muscled expanse of chest. She was determined to have the last word. "I'm not a little wanton," she murmured sleepily. *"Crystal's* the little wanton . . ."

10

CASEY STARED DOWN at the picture in the society column, studying it dispassionately. The last time she had seen that face had been a week ago over breakfast in a Boston hotel, the morning after Matt had carried her upstairs because she was too tipsy to walk. Now, seated at her desk in her office, she coolly studied the man who had brought her to such heights of ecstacy that night. What could the picture tell her about him? That he was incredibly good-looking, yes. There was no denying his potent, masculine appeal. He had the rugged good looks of an American cowboy, with a determined jaw, shaggy eyebrows, a devilish gleam in his eyes, and thick hair that was just a half-inch longer than respectable, adding to the roguish appeal of his charm.

It told her he was confident, for self-assurance radiated from the tall frame. This was no man to back down from a fight or cower in a board room. He exuded a calm sense of his own belief in himself. Energy and determination were written all over his magnificent physique.

The picture also told Casey something else about the man—that he was undeniably attractive to women. The woman in the picture with him showed this beyond any doubt. She was tall and blond and looked as if she had been born with a sterling spoon in her mouth. The dress she wore would cost most women half a year's salary. She had the aristocratic good looks of a thoroughbred—and she also had eyes only for Matt Stoner. She was glowing up at him, her head tilted provocatively, her teeth shining like pearls, her neck a slim wand circled by emeralds, her shoulders bare, displaying the tan that the write-up beneath the picture explained she had acquired in Acapulco the week before.

Casey's eyebrow arched as she studied the woman. One thing was certain, *she* hadn't grown up in South Boston. Paris, perhaps, or Chevy Chase, or Greenwich, but never a workingman's suburb like South Boston. Heaving a sigh, Casey put the article down and swiveled her chair to look out the window. She was troubled, but couldn't say exactly why. She only knew that looking at that picture had brought all sorts of doubts rushing to the surface. How could she possibly think that a man like Matt Stoner, rich, successful, enormously attractive, could ever be truly interested in her? What possible future could there be with a man like Matt? A few more gloriously beautiful nights in bed, then what? Something would happen—he would meet another woman, or get bored, or realize that Casey was from another world, with a background entirely unlike his—and then he would drift away, leaving her to try to put her life together again, minus his presence.

At that thought, Casey closed her eyes, feeling pain stab at her. What was happening to her? Surely she wasn't falling in love with Matt Stoner? Why did it bother her to think of him not ever calling again? She wasn't a schoolgirl any more, dependent on a man's attentions for her self-esteem. So why did the thought of a life without Matt Stoner leave her feeling empty? Hadn't she known from the very beginning that he wasn't for her?

Yes, but then she had thought he was a womanizing playboy. Now she knew different, despite how things looked in this picture. Even though she had given Matt a hard time about Crystal last week, she realized that she believed him. There was a depth of sincerity to Matt that she hadn't suspected on that first day when she met him. Having stumbled into his office to find him with a young girl in his arms, Casey had jumped to a wrong conclusion. Time hadn't borne that conclusion out. Her own relationship with Matt, limited though it was, had shown her another side of him, a strong, caring side. Totally and securely masculine, he could afford to be gentle. Totally confident, he could give rein to his sense of humor. The devils that gleamed in his gray eyes were amused devils, laughing at him as much as at the foibles of the world. He made her happy. He made her shiver with need. He made her laugh and feel soaring ecstacy. But how did he feel about her? Could he ever accept her background? She was from such a different world. For the last five years she had moved in wealthy circles, but there could be no denying her roots. They were firmly entrenched in the poor soil of the working-class neighborhoods of South Boston. She now served raspberry mousse and pineapple *beau rivage* for dessert, but at one time had considered chocolate ice cream the ultimate treat. Though she chose French *nouvelle cuisine* while dining out, she could clearly remember eating corned beef and cabbage, seated around a rectangular, formica-topped table with aluminum legs in a steamy kitchen filled with cooking odors and lots of love.

Biting at her lip, Casey turned back to look at the photogaraph of Matt again. Why did he have to be so devastatingly attractive? Why couldn't he have been fat and balding? Then the prospect of spending a month at his summer home wouldn't be quite so unnerving. If she felt this way about the man after only being with him four times in her entire life, what in heaven's name would happen to her if she spent every day with him?

Feeling suddenly irritable, Casey tossed the society column aside and tried to immerse herself in her work, but her thoughts persistently wandered back to Matt. When she had seen him last he had explained that he was going to New York for at least a week and that he would call her when he arrived back in Boston. Casey's eyes drifted toward the calendar on her desk. A large black nine stared up at her reproachfully. That had been a week ago, a full week of not seeing Matt but of dreaming about him at night and thinking about him all day. April ninth—a whole week! Would he come back to Boston today, or would his trip be extended? Damn the man! The least he could do was call and let her know how he was!

Overwhelmed by frustration, Casey tore the page off her calendar, crumpled it into a ball, and threw it in the waste-basket.

"Feeling better now?"

Joanie's voice startled her, and Casey looked up to see her assistant leaning against the door jamb, a faintly amused smile on her face. Grinning sheepishly, Casey took off her glasses and rubbed the bridge of her nose tiredly.

"No, not really." Gesturing for Joanie to take a seat near her desk, Casey forced a smile. It was easier to let Joanie think she was just tired from organizing the office before she left for the Cape at the end of the month. Casey's pride wouldn't allow her to admit she was miserable over a man. She spread her arms wide over the jumbled mass of papers on her desk and shrugged. "Where do I start?"

"Casey," Joanie said in a gentle voice, "it's going to be all right. I won't let you down, I promise. When you come back, everything will be just fine. Nothing will fall apart. And you need a vacation, Casey. Look at you—you're strung as tight as a fiddle."

Casey smiled ironically. She was strung tightly, but not because of worry about her business.

"I've never doubted you for a minute, Joanie," she said

reassuringly. "Don't worry about that. But you're right—I *do* need a vacation. Badly." Casey picked up a pile of papers and began leafing through them. "I've gone through all our advance orders and have pretty much planned all the menus. That phone call this morning sounded urgent, though. I'm going to meet this Mr. . . ." Casey glanced at the memo in her hand to check the name. "Mr. Davis." A frown creased her forehead. "Where have I heard that name, Joanie? Alonzo Davis. Does that sound familiar to you?"

Joanie looked up sharply. "Shipping. Something about shipping. I read his name in an article about Stefanos Christopoulis."

Casey smacked her hand on the desk. "That's it! Alonzo Davis is a rival of Stefanos Christopoulis." She smiled uncertainly. "Now isn't that a coincidence? Here it's been only a couple of weeks since I cooked a meal for one international shipping magnate and another one is on the phone asking to meet with me." She shrugged elaborately, laughing in self-mockery. "Word must be getting around."

"You know what they say," Joanie laughed in response. "When it rains it pours."

"Shipping magnates, no less." Casey shook her head at herself, then sat idly tapping her pen on the surface of her desk as Joanie fussed over another pile of papers. There really *was* something the matter with her when she couldn't place the name of a man like Alonzo Davis. Casey read the newspapers and news magazines faithfully. Familiarity with what was going on locally and nationally had always put her miles ahead of her competition. That was how she had happened on Matt's picture this morning. And that, Casey realized suddenly, was why she hadn't been able to think clearly and remember who Alonzo Davis was. Seeing Matt's picture had turned her head to mush. Any other day she would have remembered Davis's name and reacted like the crackerjack she was. Today it had taken her assistant to remember. Sighing, Casey sat back and closed her eyes. Maybe she really did need a vacation. Or maybe she just needed Matt to call.

*   *   *

The restaurant where Casey was to meet Alonzo Davis was located in the shopping mall that Matt had saved from the wrecker's ball. The mall was tucked into an old brick warehouse and it conveyed an intimate ambience, fostered by the judicious use of sandblasted brick, dark wood paneling, hanging plants, and skylights in the soaring ceilings, open to the blue April sky.

Standing in the doorway to the restaurant while she waited for the maitre d' to take her to her table, Casey was suitably impressed. This was definitely the kind of restaurant an internationally known shipping magnate might frequent. Unless, of course, he was Stefanos Christopoulis, in which case it seemed that any restaurant in Boston was out of the question.

"Ah, Mrs. Adams." Alonzo Davis stood up when she approached the table, took her hand, and raised it to his lips. "Charmed."

Casey's eyebrow rose fractionally. These continental manners took getting used to. Recovering her poise, she detached her hand from his and slid gracefully into her chair. "Mr. Davis," she murmured, nodding politely, "it's a pleasure to meet you."

His black eyes gleamed at her. "You're so very formal, Mrs. Adams. Or may I call you Casey? It's such an... American name."

Casey smiled wryly, slightly mystified by her companion. Though tall and good-looking, with dignified gray hair and smooth manners, there was something about him that wasn't quite right. "Well, I *am* an American, Mr. Davis," she said, smiling at him. "So my having an American name should hardly surprise you." She had barely finished speaking when it hit her what was bothering her about him—he was laughing at her. There was definite amusement lurking in his dark eyes. It wasn't unpleasant laughter, neither cruel, or hurtful, yet laughter all the same. She felt anger bubbling underneath her surface. "You seem to find something about me amusing, Mr. Davis. Do you mind sharing it with me? I'm always up for a good laugh."

Alonzo Davis's polite smile broadened into a grin, revealing teeth that didn't go with the rest of his debonair façade. They were large and slightly yellowed, and the front teeth were chipped. Casey looked away quickly, aware that she had been staring in surprise.

"I purposely haven't gotten my teeth capped, Mrs. Adams," he said, his voice filled with amusement. "I want to remember my humble beginnings. Something tells me that you also come from a neighborhood not as rich as this one."

Casey nodded slowly. "South Boston," she said. "And you?"

He shrugged. "London. The poorest part. I've managed to refine my voice and my manners so I can pass in the most respectable restaurants, but I can always spot someone who's not been born to it, as the expression goes."

Casey was intrigued. Hadn't she been thinking about her neighborhood only this morning? "What gave me away?" she asked.

"Nothing that anyone else would ever spot," he answered. "Except perhaps your perfectly formal manners. The really rich are so confident in themselves that they never worry about being polite." His teeth flashed yellow, as large and unsightly as an old horse's. "It's a major failing with the rich, I think."

Casey frowned. At one point in her life she might have agreed with Alonzo Davis, but now she felt his assumption was too sweeping. Matt Stoner was enormously wealthy, after all, and *he* was always polite. She smiled at Davis and shrugged. "But you're rich now, and you're polite, Mr. Davis. Your logic doesn't hold up."

"But I wasn't born to it, Casey. I made my money the hard way, like you, perhaps, and so I think I can afford to be critical of the lazy ones who inherit and do nothing to earn it." His face became implacably hard, and Casey shivered slightly. She could see how he had become as successful as he was. There was brute determination in that bland face, lurking just beneath the civilized surface. He was the kind of man who might do anything to get ahead.

There was a ruthlessness about him that made Casey feel uncomfortable. This man, though he could be charming, wasn't to be trusted. Not one inch.

As if sensing her withdrawal, Alonzo Davis took her hand and brought it to his lips again. He kissed the back of her hand, then turned her hand over and kissed the palm, his lips dry to the touch, yet opening slightly, sending a warning tremor over Casey's skin. She was about to withdraw her hand when a flash of light erupted nearby. Confused, she turned her head toward the source of the light and found herself facing a photographer. Behind him, Pamela Tyrone was studying the other diners. A small worm of discomfort twisted in Casey. What was Pamela Tyrone doing here with a photographer? At that moment Pamela spied her, and a cool smile touched her flawless face.

"Well, well, Mrs. Adams. What a surprise!"

Casey barely mustered a smile herself. She didn't know why, but she still didn't trust Pamela Tyrone. "Yes, isn't it?" she murmured.

Pamela took the photographer by the arm and approached Casey and Davis. "Kevin and I are here working on an advertising project. Matt wants a huge spread in one of the Sunday papers on the whole renovation he's done here. We're out for the day taking just scads of pictures, aren't we, Kevin?"

The photographer, who looked bored, barely nodded. Pamela's feline eye fell on Alonzo Davis. "Aren't you going to introduce me, Casey?" she asked archly.

"Pamela Tyrone, Alonzo Davis," Casey said shortly. She was in no mood to play Cupid for Pamela Tyrone, or to sit by and watch Pamela stretch out her cool palm for a lingering kiss. But Alonzo had already released Pamela's hand.

"You mentioned a man named Matt who did this renovation. Not Matt Stoner, by any chance?"

At the mention of Matt's name Casey looked up sharply, just in time to see a look pass between Davis and Pamela. Was Casey imagining things, or had it been a conspiratorial look, as if they were hatching a plot together? Staring at them, Casey decided it had been all in her imagination.

What she had witnessed had merely been two attractive people signaling their awareness of each other.

"Why, yes, as a matter of fact," Pamela was saying, "I did mean Matt Stoner." There was quiet amusement in her cool blue eyes. "And if you're the Alonzo Davis I think you are, you have good reason to dislike Matt right about now."

Davis laughed. "Not really. All's fair in love and war, as they say. If he deals with Christopoulis, it will be his eventual loss and then he'll come to me." A snake's smile crossed his handsome face. "I can wait."

Casey frowned. What were they talking about? How did Alonzo Davis know about Matt and Stefanos Christopoulis? And why did she suddenly feel ill at ease, as if she were dining in the enemy's camp? Had Alonzo Davis somehow gotten word that she had cooked a meal for Matt and Christopoulis and asked her here to pump her for information? If so, then he would be sadly disappointed. Casey made it a point to never share information she happened on in the course of her work. And because of her strong feelings for Matt Stoner, she was doubly determined not to do anything that might adversely affect his dealings with Stefanos Chrisopoulis. Matt had trusted her to cook the meal that won him Christopoulis's promise to negotiate further. She wasn't going to repay his trust by doing anything that might harm him in any way.

Pamela had turned back to Casey. "Well, Mrs. Adams, enjoy your meal." She glanced meaningfully at Davis, then returned her gaze to Casey. "How interesting that you should be here with Stefanos Christopoulis's arch business enemy." She smiled coolly. "But then I suppose you'd work for anyone, if the price were right, Mrs. Adams."

Casey felt as if someone had turned cold air on her. Something about Pamela's tone of voice, about the implications that drifted underneath her words, chilled Casey. She couldn't put her finger on the reason, but she felt vaguely frightened, as if a subtle threat had been thrown out to her by Pamela Tyrone.

Summoning her most cordial smile, Casey inclined her

head. "It was pleasant seeing you again, Pamela," she said, dismissing her, then turning to study the menu. When she was sure Pamela was gone, she raised her head and saw Alonzo Davis studying her with calculating eyes.

"And how do you know Miss Tyrone?" he asked.

"I've worked for her boss," Casey answered shortly.

"You mean for Matt Stoner, I presume."

Casey felt suddenly irritated. She was here to discuss the possibility of working for Alonzo Davis, not her past history of work contracts. "Since her boss is Matt Stoner," she said sharply, "then that's who I mean."

"Ah, now I've angered you, Mrs. Adams." Alonzo Davis reached for her hand. "What must I do to restore your previous good temper?"

Casey withdrew her hand. "Perhaps if we concentrate on business, I'll no longer be angry. How does that sound?" she asked, throwing him a cool glance.

Davis took the hint with easy grace. "Very well, business it will be." He propped his elbows on the table and studied her with those unnerving black eyes. "I have a home in the Bahamas, Mrs. Adams, and next month will be spending a great deal of time there, after sailing my yacht from Boston Harbor. My usual cook has suddenly quit, and I'm left with the prospect of no one to feed my guests. I've heard of you and thought I'd approach you with an offer. A month in the Bahamas, Mrs. Adams, at a very attractive fee."

Bemused, Casey could only stare at him. What was going on in her usual dull life? First she had an invitation to go to the Cape for the month of May, and now she was getting one to spend the month in the Bahamas.

"Next month?" she repeated, wishing he meant the month of June instead.

"That's right," he nodded pleasantly. "The month of May. I'll be sailing from Boston Harbor with a few guests on my yacht." His eyes took on a slightly suggestive look. "You're welcome to come along on the yacht, if you like, or you can fly down and meet me there."

If she hadn't seen that gleam of barely restrained sexual innuendo in Alonzo Davis's eyes, Casey might have been

tempted to say yes. After all, the Bahamas in May would
certainly be more exciting than Cape Cod. But Casey had
no desire to fend off the advances of Alonzo Davis on a
ship, where she would be trapped without any way to get
off. And besides, she had already agreed to work for Matt.
Spending a month with Matt anywhere, even in Hoboken,
was infinitely preferable to spending a month with Alonzo
Davis, even if it were in the most posh resort in the Carib-
bean.

"I'm afraid I've already made plans for the month of
May, Mr. Davis. I'd be happy to recommend one of my
staff to you, though."

He was reaching for her hand again, stroking it lightly,
his dark eyes gleaming into hers. "Are you sure I can't
convince you, Mrs. Adams?" he asked softly.

With cool determination she withdrew her hand. You've
just convinced me, Mr. Davis, she thought with a touch of
annoyance, but smiled and shook her head. "I'm afraid not,
Mr. Davis, but let me give you the names of two of my
finest chefs."

Casey was still at her desk, inundated with work, when
her phone rang at six thirty. She stabbed the blinking button
with one finger and lifted the receiver, her mind still occupied with the plans for a wedding.

"Casey Adams."

"Matt Stoner." His deep voice was tinged with humor,
as if he were mocking her professional manner.

Immediately Casey felt a surge of elation. The tiredness
that had been dogging her since her meeting with Alonzo
Davis disappeared, replaced by an incredible rush of well-
being. He was back! He had called! Damn the man for
making her miserable for a week and then elevating her to
heaven by a mere phone call! It might be illogical, but she
was going to make him pay for it. She wasn't going to fall
into his lap like a peach ripe for the plucking.

Sitting back, she took off her glasses and swung them
back and forth in her hand. "Well, well. If it isn't the
lonesome stranger just blown into town."

He chuckled softly. "Howdy, partner."

"Who says?"

"Oh ho! Stay away a week and you go getting all independent on me."

"I wasn't aware that I was ever anything *but* independent, Mr. Stoner." Her eyes were twinkling as she spoke, and she knew he could tell.

"Mrs. Adams, I'm in no mood to spar with you. I've just gotten back from an exhausting week in New York, and I'm in the mood for a steak dinner, a shower, and some good loving, not necessarily in that order, so why don't you hustle out to Logan and let's get down to business."

"What kind of business, Mr. Stoner? Funny business or monkey business?"

"Serious business, Casey Adams," he answered grimly. "I mean it when I say I'm tired. Waging a battle of wits with you isn't exactly my idea of a good time."

"What is? Going to discos with...oh, what was her name?" Casey fished around in the wastebasket for the society column she had thrown out earlier. "Ah, yes. Angela Hardwick, just back from sunning herself in Acapulco."

A heavy sigh came through the receiver. "My past always seems to catch up with me."

"So does your present."

"Angela Hardwick is definitely out of my past. I just happened to meet up with her—"

"And asked her to go out dancing," Casey finished for him. "That's entirely logical, Matthew—just like breaking in poor little Crystal Fensterwick."

"Casey. I'm at Logan Airport. I'm tired, I'm hungry, and damn it, I want you like hell. Now get that body of yours out here or I'll tan your hide when I get to you. Is that clear?"

She thought of answering "crystal clear," but managed not to. What she did was murmur "yes," and then drive to Logan Airport as if the Little People from Ireland were after her.

11

CASEY STARED DOWN at the piece of paper in her hand, wondering if she could have possibly misunderstood the directions to Matt Stoner's Cape Cod home. But no, the directions were so simple, and she had followed them faithfully.

Lifting troubled eyes, she gazed at the impressive white-clapboard mansion that stood in front of the sweeping semi-circular drive. Her small car was swamped by the surroundings. The house itself was mammoth—three stories high, with sparkling twelve-over-twelve colonial windows, a huge double door surmounted by a gracious fanlight, and double chimneys sprouting from the slate roof.

A tall black wrought-iron fence surrounded the property

by the road, but that was lost from sight, screened by masses of flowering shrubs, pines, and maples. Nothing stirred. All was peaceful. Then gradually Casey's city-accustomed ears picked up the chatter of robins as they hopped from branch to branch in the surrounding trees, the gentle murmur of wind among the leaves, the far-off barking of a dog.

And the smells! Casey lifted her head and breathed in the delicious tang of salt air. It mingled with the scents of tulips, daffodils, and hyacinths which were planted in broad beds that lined the vivid green of the lawn.

But then the front door swung open and Casey forgot her surroundings. Yes, this was Matt's home, for there was Pamela Tyrone, standing in the doorway, looking every inch the beautiful hostess. Faced as she was by the fashion plate in front of her, Casey was pitifully aware of her own wrinkled, faded jeans and baggy crewneck sweater. Pamela wore a shocking-pink linen dress, so simple that it must have cost a small fortune. The pearls that circled her neck looked suspiciously real. The slim, high-heeled sandals she wore made her feet look frail and terribly feminine, so unlike the sneakers that Casey had put on, thinking only of comfort on her long drive down from Boston.

Casey sighed inwardly and put on a bright smile as she advanced toward the door. Nothing much had changed, she saw, fighting an ironic grin. Pamela's eyes were as glacial as ever. That fact alone almost made Casey feel at home.

"You found us, I see," Pamela said, her cool voice drifting toward Casey along with a cloud of expensive perfume.

"Yes, the directions were foolproof." Casey stopped at the bottom step. "You look all settled in." She had made a statement, but inside it was a question. For some reason Casey felt uneasy. Something didn't feel right. She had expected Matt to come running out to meet her. She had expected a small, silver-shingled cottage with a picket fence and two or three tiny bedrooms. And most of all, she had not expected Pamela Tyrone to open the door to this impressive mansion, looking every inch at home and in command.

"Oh my, yes," Pamela answered haughtily, "Matt and I

came down yesterday—to get things in order, you know."

Yes, Matt had told Casey he was leaving yesterday. For the past three weeks he had spent much of his free time with her, and their relationship had grown. Casey's fears that there could be no future with Matt had dwindled, held at bay by his constant presence and by the look in his gray eyes when he made love to her.

But now, looking around, Casey felt the fears returning. It was one thing to live in an impressive townhouse in Beacon Hill. It was another entirely to own a summer home so huge and impressive that most people could only dream of having it as a year-round home. And hadn't he mentioned a condominium in Mexico and a ski chalet in Vermont?

"And where is Mr. Stoner?" Casey asked brightly.

"Matt's tied up, I'm afraid," Pamela said smoothly. "He's asked me to show you to your quarters." She shut the door behind her and gestured for Casey to follow her.

"My quarters?" Casey asked, forcing a laugh. "You make it sound as though I'm a servant, Pam."

A mocking smile glinted in Pamela's eyes. "Well, you *are* the original Maid To Order, aren't you?"

Casey felt a chill shiver across her skin and decided it must be the cool Cape air. She would have to remember to wear a light jacket when she was outdoors.

The path they followed took them around the side of the house to the back, where they passed a flower-bordered brick terrace and plunged even further into a densely shaded tree-lined path that led down a gently sloping hill, toward a small cottage.

"This is where you'll be staying," Pamela said when they reached it. "It's small and rather crude, but it should be suitable."

Casey forced a smile, all the time trying to make sense of everything. Why had Matt put her down here, so far away from everyone else? It didn't make sense.

But once inside the cottage, Casey's questions evaporated. It was charming! It was exactly what she had imagined when she thought of Matt's summer home. There were overstuffed chintz-covered chairs and sofas, and a fieldstone fireplace where white birch logs waited to chase away the mid-spring chill. On either side of the fireplace were French doors that led to a small brick terrace. Far below it was Woods Hole Harbor. A small bedroom opened off the living room. It was simply furnished with a white antique iron bed with a blue-and-white patchwork quilt and a frilly eyelet dust ruffle and pillow shams. Gaily colored rag rugs covered the buttery pine floor, and ruffled curtains hung at spotlessly clean windows. There was a white wooden bureau and a white antique wicker rocking chair. A small bathroom, clean and sparkling, was just off the bedroom.

The kitchen was also small and narrow, with white cabinets and a blue tiled floor. A tiny window over the sink looked toward the distant harbor.

Casey spun toward Pamela. "Why, I love it! It's just perfect!"

Pamela smiled coolly. "We thought you'd feel at home here. It's where we normally put our guests' servants."

Casey's high spirits plummeted as Pamela's words resurrected her fears.

She spun away, her back to Pamela as she looked out the tiny kitchen window. Wasn't this what she had told herself in the first place? That Matt and she could have no future together because their backgrounds were so different? In Boston, where she ran a successful business and dressed like the other women on Beacon Hill, their differences had not seemed as important. But here, on this impressive and elegant estate, Casey stood out for what she was—a maid, someone hired to cook the meals, fit only for servants' quarters.

Summoning her courage, Casey took a breath and turned back to Pamela. "Thank you for showing me around, Miss Tyrone. I'll get my bags and unpack."

"No need to worry about cooking tonight, Mrs. Adams," Pamela said. "Mary O'Reilly is here and will make supper this evening. There's food in the cupboards here, so you can do for yourself, I presume. You're to be at the kitchens by six tomorrow morning. Is that clear, Mrs. Adams?"

In just a few words, Pamela Tyrone had devastatingly

reduced her to the status of a servant. Lifting her chin, Casey smiled serenely. "Perfectly clear, Miss Tyrone."

After Pamela left, it took Casey two hours to get her suitcases unpacked. Then, feeling chilly, she lit the fireplace and fixed a drink, but that hadn't been enough to chase the tension from her limbs. The entire conversation with Pamela Tyrone kept echoing in her mind. Why *had* Matt put her in this cottage? After she had used some energy unpacking, things had seemed simpler to her—it wasn't because he thought of her as a servant, but because he wanted her to have a place of her own. Or perhaps he thought she would be more comfortable here. But then the same doubts returned. *Why* had he thought she'd be more comfortable here? Because he knew she would never fit in on a social level with all his rich friends? Had he realized already what she had only feared? That she was fine working for the rich, but couldn't ever join them at their tables?

When the doubts and fears had churned her stomach and muscles to unbearable anxiety, she drew a hot bath, then slid into the frothy luxury. She had tied her hair on top of her head, but already the steam of the bath was causing tiny tendrils to escape and curl about her face.

Slowly the hot water began to work its restorative magic. Her skin grew pink from the heat, her muscles began to loosen, and her eyes grew drowsy. She was completely relaxed, her mind a calm blank. But at the sound of a floorboard squeaking, she sat up, her breasts rising out of the bubbly soapsuds, the pink nipples just visible.

There it was again, that same sound. As if someone were walking very stealthily in the living room, approaching the small bedroom. But she had locked the front door, hadn't she? Long years of living alone in Boston had ingrained that habit in her—always lock the doors. But now she was no longer in her own apartment where she felt safe and secure. It hit her suddenly just how alone she was. She was quite far, really, from the main house. If she were to scream, if she were to *need* to scream, no one would even hear her.

A chill feathered across her skin. The bath water had gotten cold, that was why, she told herself. But another voice challenged her, telling her that no, those really were footsteps, and they were in the bedroom, heading for the bathroom. . . .

The door swung open and Casey screamed. Without thinking, she lifted the large loofah sponge, dripping with water, and swung it with all her might at the tall male figure that appeared in the doorway. The sponge landed with pinpoint precision, smack in the middle of Matt Stoner's face.

A combination of relief and humor hit Casey at the same time. Collapsing into laughter, she felt herself go weak. "Matt," she screeched when she could find her voice. "Oh, thank goodness it's you! I thought it was a burglar!" She stopped laughing, took one look at his dripping face, and started up again. Matt stood unmoving, soapy water dripping down his face.

"When you're finished laughing, Mrs. Adams," he said with deadly calm, "perhaps we can discuss your unreasonable fears."

Casey put a hand to her mouth to hide her quivering lips. He really did look a bit silly, standing there like an enraged bull, soaking wet. Her lips just didn't want to stop laughing, but she really mustn't give in. Matt Stoner's considerable dignity had been badly bruised, and she knew she was treading on dangerous ground. Still the humor refused to be banished. Her cheeks burned as she fought to control her rebellious lips.

"You really do look quite funny, Matt," she murmured.

His gray eyes looked like a windswept sea. They traveled her lazily, taking in the hair that was trailing over her shoulders, then dipping to the lush curves of her breasts, stopping to feast on the pink-tipped nipples that stood erect in the center of the ivory mounds.

"Are you cold, Mrs. Adams?" he asked.

"Cold?" She shrugged one shoulder. "Not particularly. Why?"

"Because your nipples are hard. That happens sometimes, I hear, when a lady gets chilled."

Hot color swept into her cheeks. After sharing a bed with the man for almost a month, you'd think he wouldn't be able to embarrass her, but he still could! Damn him! He was capable of reducing her to shaking chagrin. She felt raw and exposed. Hoping to rescue her own dignity, she slipped lower into the water.

"The water *is* beginning to cool down a bit," she said softly, unable to meet his eyes. "I guess I am a little chilly."

"Then perhaps I should warm you up," he suggested.

That tone of voice warned her. She knew him well enough by now to know that when he sounded drowsy and slightly amused, he was ready to pounce. Irritation flared through her. What right did he have to unlock her home—it *was* hers now, would be for the next month—and walk in un- invited? He had scared her silly, and if she had reacted by throwing a wet sponge at him and thereby wounding his precious dignity, then that was just too bad for him. He was lucky she hadn't thrown something harder. That huge jar of bath salts, for instance. And furthermore, there was this matter of him sticking her down here in the first place!

"I'm warm enough, thank you," she said stiffly, tilting her chin at a defiant angle, still not looking at him.

"Not from the way you sound, you're not."

An action caught the corner of Casey's eye. She turned to find him unbuttoning his shirt. Angrily she sat up, only to remember her nakedness and plunge under the water again.

"*What* do you think you're doing?" she demanded.

"Taking off my shirt."

Her eyes flicked venomously toward him, then widened. "That's not your shirt!" she snapped, watching him unbuckle his belt and unzip his fly.

"Very observant, Casey," he murmured dryly. He sat down on the toilet seat and pulled off one trouser leg, then the other, then stood up and shucked off his underwear. Casey stared. There was no getting around it, he had the most beautiful body she had ever seen. All smooth, rippling muscles, totally masculine—so different from hers—hard and massive and unyielding. And aroused. Her eyes shifted away uncomfortably. Undoubtedly aroused.

She tried to keep the anger in her voice, but other feelings were swamping her. "And what's the purpose exactly?" she asked, knowing that her voice sounded breathless, betraying her own state of arousal.

"I like to take my baths naked," he explained, approaching her.

"Then I'll just get out and drain the water and draw you another," she said sweetly, certain that wasn't what he had in mind. And she was glad. She felt herself trembling all over at the thought of what was going to happen.

He was at the edge of the tub now. If she turned her head, she would be looking directly at a highly impassioned man. Flame-faced, she decided to stare straight ahead.

"Would you like me to sit facing you or get in behind you?" Matt asked pleasantly.

She swallowed, knowing that her pulse was beating erratically in her neck and knowing that he must be watching it, smiling at how it betrayed her. "Neither," she whispered.

"Next to you?" he asked incredulously. "There's not enough room, Casey darling. These old tubs just weren't built to accommodate lovers."

Unable to think of a response, she brought her knees up and circled them with her arms, resting her chin on them as she bit at her lip. What did other women do in this situation? Why wasn't she sophisticated? Why didn't she just *know* what to say and do?

"I think I'll get in behind," Matt said softly, and then there was no escape. His strong legs swung over the side of the tub and settled down on either side of her, and his muscular arms came around her from behind, pulling her back against his chest. His palms cupped her breasts, and he began massaging her still-aroused nipples.

"Feels nice, hmmm?" he murmured, his lips playing at the side of her neck.

She felt strangely weightless, swamped by sensuous longings and physical need. Her body felt as if it were on fire. She was breathless, quivering with desire. She could only nod, arching her neck sideways to allow his lips to plunder the soft curve that joined neck to shoulder.

"Mmmm," she murmured breathlessly. "It's very nice."

One of his hands slid lower, and she arched back against him, a tiny moan escaping from her lips. "Matt..."

"I want to make love to you," he said, his voice low and demanding next to her ear.

"Here?" she breathed.

His low chuckle filled her ears. "Yes, here, you silly little darling."

"But..." she swallowed convulsively. "How?"

His hands slid even lower. "Trust me, Casey," he murmured. "And I'll show you...."

The next morning Casey appeared in the kitchen before six o'clock. She did a quick inventory of the utensils and food supplies, got reacquainted with Mary O'Reilly, and commandeered a small desk in an alcove off the kitchen for herself. Here she would sit and plan the day's menus, make out the shopping lists, go over the kitchen accounts, and keep track of wine supplies. She would check the linen supplies and order fresh flowers. And here, seated at this small desk, with the window facing the long stretch of lawn that led to the harbor far below, she would dream of Matt.

Last night's lovemaking had eased her doubts completely. He had been ardent, demanding, and gently passionate. From the tub he had carried her to the bed and cradled her in his strong arms, stroking her tumbled hair while whispering endearments to her. How could she have ever doubted his feelings for her? That wasn't the way a man treated a servant. There had been tender, loving emotion in his every action. And they had lain in the bed for hours, talking easily, laughing gently, murmuring, caressing each other, feeling at peace.

Casey glanced at the clock, excitement mounting at the prospect of seeing Matt. It was almost eight o'clock, time for the guests to begin stirring for breakfast. And just before he had slipped from her bed last night, Matt had told her he wanted her to join him and his guests at meals. So she would be expected to dine with the guests—what further evidence did she need to know that he wasn't ashamed of her, that he hadn't tucked her away in the small cottage because she wasn't good enough?

The dining room was a symphony of blue and white. French doors stood open to a brick terrace, admitting the early sunshine along with the tang of salt air and the gossip of the birds as they twittered in the trees. The walls were covered in a simple blue-and-white-striped wallpaper, and the windows were curtainless. A round glass-topped dining table sat in the middle of the room. Five places were set with white ironstone dishes, bowls of fruit, and platters of sausage, bacon, eggs, ham, and corn and blueberry muffins. Mugs of hot coffee sat steaming at each place, and Casey had found the time to sneak out into the garden and gather a bouquet of daffodils and tulips for the center of the table. White Chippendale-style chairs with blue cushions surrounded the table, inviting the guests to make themselves comfortable.

Casey could barely keep the green sparks from flying from her eyes as she joined Stefanos, Anna Copeland, and Pamela Tyrone. When Matt entered the room, dressed in faded jeans and a striped T-shirt, her heart somersaulted with joy at seeing him. He looked so different from the man she was used to. No three-piece suits here. Instead, he was the epitome of the casual man, his broad shoulders and muscular chest emphasized by the well-fitting shirt, his trim waist and abdomen even more manifest in the faded, tight jeans.

Casey met his eyes with a warm smile, only to receive a cool nod from him. Startled and a little hurt, she ducked her head, picked up her spoon quickly, and dipped it into the bowl of melon and strawberries. After a night spent in such wonderful lovemaking, she had expected more than a casual nod from him. A smile would have been enough. Some kind of special look. A murmured good morning. . . .

Raising her eyes, Casey tried to get Matt's attention. Perhaps she had somehow misinterpreted his action. But no, he was deeply engrossed in conversation with Stefanos

Christopoulis, ignoring her completely. Miffed, Casey attacked her fruit, then realized she had no appetite. On her other side Pamela Tyrone and Anna Copeland were laughing easily about some story Anna was relating about working on a Hollywood set. Casey tried to listen to the story, but she had joined in too late and the gist of it was lost to her. Growing increasingly uncomfortable, she waited to join the conversation at an appropriate time, but never seemed to find one. Was it her imagination, or was Pamela Tyrone deliberately excluding her? Every time Anna Copeland looked toward Casey with a gesture to include her, Pamela seemed to intervene, drawing Anna's attention back to herself. And as for Matt, he was so absorbed with Stefanos that a small earthquake might have shaken the house from its very foundation and he wouldn't have noticed.

By the time breakfast was over, Casey felt two red spots of indignation burning in her cheeks. She was thankful that no one seemed to notice. They were still all too intent on each other to pay her any mind. Scraping back her chair, she made her way to the kitchen and her small desk. Her eyes were unseeing as she stared out the window toward the blue expanse of water far below.

Now what was she to think? Were her worst fears all true, then? Had it all come about as she had worried it would? Was she the paid help, invited to sit at her master's table, but ignored because she just wasn't good enough to participate in the social life of the ultrarich?

12

IN THE TWO weeks that followed, Casey's confidence returned. In observing Matt, she saw that he was completely occupied with his negotiations with Stefanos. At first put out by this, wanting to be the center of his existence, she soon realized that she was being unreasonable. Matt was here on business, trying to consummate a deal that would ultimately bring him enormous financial rewards, not to mention the praise he would earn from the United States government in securing a contract that would bring added security to world trade.

And if he didn't spend every night with her, if he and Stefanos retired to the study to talk until past midnight, he did spend some nights with her. His lovemaking was as

ardent and passionate as ever, even perhaps more so. There
was an added dimension to it, something that Casey wasn't
quite capable of putting her finger on, but which brought a
glow to her cheeks when she thought of it. She supposed
it had something to do with how they talked together. She
told Matt about how she had started her business and how
she might expand it now that she was such a success in
Boston. He shared his concerns, asked her opinions, confided his doubts. To Casey, the discovery that the seemingly
all-confident Matthew Stoner had doubts was a revelation.
But when she thought about it more carefully, she realized
that she too seemed very confident, yet was persistently
bothered by nagging fears about Matt's feelings for her,
about her ability to fit into his lifestyle.

And so, in an effort to struggle with her questions, she
took long drives around the Cape. Her duties, once she
established a routine, were minimal. Mary O'Reilly was
entirely capable of carrying out most of her instructions.
Casey herself prepared very few meals, although she planned
the menus, ordered the food, chose the wines, and arranged
the flowers on the table. The rest of her time was her own.
Because Matt was tied up with Stefanos all day, her trips
around the Cape became an everyday occurrence. She toured
the small center of Woods Hole, then drove to nearby Falmouth and poked around the shops. She spent one entire
day in Hyannis and others driving slowly along the winding
back roads that stretched from Woods Hole all the way to
the tip of the Cape at Provincetown. And all the while she
thought about her growing feelings for Matthew Stoner.
What had started out as explosive physical attraction had
deepened. At first, seeing Matt Stoner in his office with
Crystal Fensterwick, Casey had assumed Matt to be the
typical rich playboy, out for all the physical pleasure he
could get, at the expense of every pretty girl who crossed
his path. But that assumption hadn't stopped her from being
attracted to him. From that first day she went to his house
to inventory his kitchen, she had been undeniably drawn to
him. Even while trying to talk sense to herself, to tell herself

to steer clear of this carouser, she had felt the attraction spreading through her body like heat through warm coals. Their lovemaking had been as dynamic as it had promised to be, but Casey puzzled over the exact point at which she began to actually *like* Matt Stoner. She thought it was at the hotel in Boston, when he carried her to that room and ministered to her in her hungover state, and then explained his relationship with Crystal. And from her own shrewd observation of him with Crystal and her mother, Casey believed him without a doubt. And with that belief came a startling discovery. She did like the man and, yes, respected him. And now, sitting on a bench on a public beach in South Yarmouth, the gulls squawking raucously overhead, the gentle lap of waves slapping against a breakwater, Casey faced something that she had been hiding from for quite some time. Matt Stoner was more to her than a casual lover, someone to enjoy in bed. Matt Stoner was—oh, face it, Casey—Matt Stoner was the man she loved.

Casey returned to Matt's house to find him, Stefanos, and Anna enjoying cocktails on the back terrace. It was an unusually warm day for mid-May. The sky was incredibly blue, the sun more a shining, golden presence than actually visible as a round ball in the sky. The trees were budding into faint green leaves, the azaleas and early rhododendrons were a riot of color. Occasional wisps of cottonlike clouds drifted overhead, and a calm breeze ruffled the foliage.

"Ah, Casey Adams!" Stefanos Christopoulis boomed out when he spied her. "Do you know what I've been day-dreaming about?"

Casey poured herself a glass of iced tea from a frosted pitcher and sank into a lawn chair. "I haven't the foggiest, Stefanos. Great big frigates or steamers or whatever you call those ugly things?" Her green eyes laughed companionably into his.

"They're called tankers," he explained patiently, a wisp of a smile on his usually stern lips. "But, no. Actually, I've been thinking about dinner tonight."

Casey grinned. "And I suppose you have your heart set on something impossible for me to come up with?"

"Not at all! You know I love everything you serve." He faked a wounded look and rubbed his stomach. "No, I've been thinking about either lobster or crabmeat. Or maybe scallops. Or fried clams with tartar sauce and a big juicy slab of lemon alongside, and those strange potatoes—French fried?"

"French *fries*," Anna corrected him. "And you know they give you indigestion."

"Not if Casey Adams cooked them," Stefanos said staunchly.

Casey glanced toward Matt and felt warmth immediately spread through her midsection. He was lolling easily in a chair, watching her with gentle eyes, a small smile playing at the corners of his chiseled mouth. (How she loved that mouth!) Shifting in his chair, Matt glanced at Stefanos. "So you admit that it's Casey's cooking that's keeping you here, eh, Stefanos?"

"I admit it," the burly man answered. "You know I've fallen for your lovely Mrs. Adams. If it weren't for Anna here, I'd try to steal her from you."

Matt reached into his pocket for one of his thin cigars. "Casey's not stealable. She's all mine—lock, stock, and barrel."

Casey's eyebrow rose in comic protest, even as a flood of tender love poured into her. "Hey! Wait just a darned minute! You talk as if you own me, *Mr.* Stoner."

Matt's eyes grinned at her from behind his hands, which cupped a match to his cigar. "Does that bother you, Casey? I thought all women wanted to feel they're wanted."

"Wanted, yes," Casey said spiritedly, "but owned, never." She tossed her mahogany hair. "This *is* the modern era, you realize."

"And you're a very modern women, aren't you?" Matt asked softly.

"Very modern, Mr. Stoner," Casey answered, her chin lifting to a defiant angle. She might just have admitted to herself a couple hours ago that she loved this man, but she was darned if she would let him know it. Even though her love for him was burning in her heart, she didn't really know how he felt for her, and she wasn't about to fall at his feet, conquered. She chided herself for acting childishly, but was determined that he would never know the extent of her feelings for him until he himself revealed his own for her. If it turned out he didn't love her, then she wanted to be able to escape, dignity intact.

At that moment Casey had the uncomfortable feeling that she was being watched. Glancing around, she realized that Pamela Tyrone had slipped unnoticed onto the terrace to join the small group. She was seated off to the side and was watching Casey, her cool blue eyes filled with amused contempt. Casey felt a shiver go over her and wished she had brought a sweater along. But inside she knew that it wasn't the cool Cape air that had chilled her, but the sudden and sure knowledge that Pamela Tyrone had looked into Casey's mind in some strange way and seen what she was thinking.

Shifting her gaze to the harbor, Casey schooled her features to remain serene. What did it matter that Pamela had realized that Casey loved Matt? Or that Casey was afraid Matt didn't return her love? Pamela Tyrone was in no position to hurt her in any way. Casey just must remember that and remember, too, that Pamela Tyrone, for all her cool and refined good looks, was just as much a servant here as she was.

That evening at dinner Anna brought conversation to a halt with the calm announcement that she had read in the local paper that Alonzo Davis had been seen strolling the streets of Provincetown.

Stefanos Christopoulis's face purpled. "Davis!" he roared. "That pirate!"

Casey kept her eyes on her plate. For some reason she didn't think it was a good idea to let anyone know that she had met with Davis. Then Casey remembered. Pamela knew she had met with him.

Casey raised her eyes to find Pamela staring at her, her

blue eyes glacial, one sleek eyebrow rising in an ironic curve. A slow, threatening smile crossed Pamela's perfect features, sending a chill over Casey's skin. But this was absurd! What was she afraid of? She had merely met with the man over luncheon to discuss the possibility of working for him. Pamela's ugly look, her implied insinuation, could mean nothing. Nevertheless, when Pamela lowered her eyes and resumed eating her meal, Casey breathed a sigh of relief. Stefanos was still ranting about Alonzo Davis, about how the man had used any means in the past to undermine his business dealings, how he wouldn't trust him for a second, about Davis's complete contempt for ethical business dealings. . . .

Matt was listening with good-humored amusement. He had no doubt grown used to the volatile temper of the Greek and knew enough to let him rave on. Anna studied her perfect, scarlet-tipped fingers and yawned, her pink mouth revealing pearl-white teeth. Casey pushed her lobster around her plate and wished she had never heard the name Alonzo Davis. What had started out as an enjoyable meal was fast deteriorating into a one-man shouting match.

Adept at smoothing things over in her business dealings, Casey stepped into the breach. "Now, Stefanos," she murmured, smiling charmingly, "I'm sure this Mr. Davis isn't all you make him out to be. He sounds like he has a hook for a hand and eats little children."

Stefanos turned his temper-blotched face toward Casey and eyed her threateningly, then seemed to make a conscious decision. Slowly the color in his face receded. He put his napkin on the table and rubbed his stomach worriedly. "Well, one thing's for sure," he said grudgingly. "The bastard's not worth ruining one of your perfect meals over."

Casey's eyes gleamed at the look on Stefanos's face. "But it looks like he's done just that. I'll have to have a talk with this Mr. Davis when I run into him on my jaunts around the Cape." What she had meant as a joke was pounced on by Stefanos.

"You know him?" he demanded.

Casey's eyes widened. What had she gotten herself into? If she explained that she *did* know him, mightn't Stefanos suspect her of having given away business secrets to him? But how could she deny knowing him, when Pamela was sitting across from her, eying her knowingly? She settled on an innocuous, evasive reply: "It was a joke, Stefanos," she said, laughing softly. "Just a joke. . . ."

At that point, Matt stood up and put an end to the conversation. "Stefanos, I imagine you'll be going to your room to rummage around in that trunk you carry for a dozen or so antacids. I think it's best if we cancel the discussions we had scheduled for tonight and resume them in the morning." His eyes drifted around the table, seeing everyone's approval, then settled on Casey. "And I am going to escort Mrs. Adams home and perhaps enjoy a stroll down to the harbor."

With that he pulled Casey's chair out, took her arm at the elbow, and ushered her out the French doors onto the patio. When he had closed the doors behind him, he turned to Casey with a grin.

"He gets worked up, doesn't he?"

But Casey wasn't thinking about Matt's question. She was remembering instead the look on Pamela Tyrone's face. The cunning, conniving look of a stalking tiger waiting for its prey to make one false move.

With an effort, Casey shook off the mental image. Cocking her head to look up at Matt, she smiled warmly. "I'm sorry—I was off in dreamland. What did you say?"

He shook his head and guided her toward the path that led to her cottage. "Nothing important."

They walked in companionable silence until they reached the bend in the path where rhododendrons screened the cottage from the main house. There Matt paused, turning to Casey and running his hands up her arms to settle on her shoulders.

"I don't see enough of you, Casey Adams. Where is this month going? When I invited you here I had visions of seeing you every day and every night. I'm beginning to wonder if this contract with Christopoulis is worth the price I'm paying."

Casey laughed throatily. "The price you're paying, Mr. Stoner?" She tilted her head provocatively. "And just what is that?"

His hands traveled slowly down her arms to catch her wrists. Roughly he pulled her against his chest, letting his lips roam her face at will. "This," he murmured huskily. "I'm not getting enough of this." His hands released her, only to pull her closer into his arms, his lips plundering hers. "Or this," he whispered, his breath fanning her parted lips as his hand came up to cup the ripe curve of her breast. "Or this...."

Primitive longings swept through Casey. The feel of his hand on her breast was as new to her as it had been the first time. She shook with need, clinging to the large male frame, her skirt whipped around her legs by the night breeze, her hair drifting like a cloud around her face. Trembling, she lifted her lips, opening them to his voracious kiss, feeling a shaft of searing passion stab her abdomen and spiral downward, pulsing in wild rhythm. Their lips broke apart then came together again, needier this time, hungrier, tongues intertwining in a primitive mating dance as their bodies pressed together, trying to merge.

Matt's strong hands bit into the soft flesh of her upper arms. "Come on," he grated. "Let's go to bed."

Casey followed him wordlessly, feeling no need to speak. Around them the pine trees and rhododendrons shifted in the night breeze, and far away the waves crashed against the shore. Overhead, pinpricks of light dotted the black velvet of the sky. The cottage itself was outlined in the glow of the outside lantern. The windows shed a warm light from the lamps that Casey had left burning.

At the door, Matt took out his key, then hesitated. Turning her head quizzically, Casey studied him. "What?" she asked, knowing intuitively that he was about to say something important.

He gazed at her, then shook his head and turned back

to the lock. "Nothing," he murmured. "I'll tell you some other time."

Feeling frustrated, as if something infinitely precious had been lost, Casey pressed him, covering her avid interest with laughter. "What?" she insisted. "Tell me. What were you going to say?"

But the door was open and he was drawing her inside, into the warm shelter of his arms as he shoved the door shut.

"Nothing," he murmured, his lips already finding her racing pulse. "Some other time." His tongue traveled in warm pathways to her ear. Shivering, she pressed against him, glorying in the feel of his body, of the hard muscles that bunched and shifted in his back as he bent to pick her up. She felt lightheaded as he swirled her into his arms and headed for the bedroom. The chintz-covered sofa swam past her, lit by the parchment-covered lamps, and then the door loomed ahead, kicked open by Matt, then kicked shut again so that the bedroom was suddenly enclosed in total darkness. Somehow he found his way to the bed, and she was swirling again, being lowered onto the soft mattress, her body quickly covered by his.

"Casey," he murmured, his lips hovering over hers. "Casey Adams."

She fought the darkness, straining to see him. Slowly her eyes focused and she could make out his image above her. Reaching up, she circled his neck with her arms. "What is it, Matthew Stoner?" she whispered.

He seemed on the brink of saying something, then once again retreated, repeating her name over and over as his lips began their slow adoration of her body. His fingers loosened buttons and clasps, slipped off clothing, and then found her softest, most vulnerable spots, where his feathered, soft caresses made her moan with need.

But then, as his body settled onto hers, the passion that had burned in them changed magically, ebbing into sweetness. Matt levered himself up onto one elbow and cupped her face tenderly with his hand, gazing down at her with warm eyes. Casey felt filled with golden light, as if somewhere deep inside Matt had ignited a bonfire of love. The caresses that before had been tempestuous were now soft, filled with warmth and shaking need.

He entered her slowly, lovingly, whispering her name. Sliding her arms around his muscled back, Casey gave herself completely to her love.

"Oh, Matt," she murmured, shaking with the golden sweetness that filled her. "Oh, Matthew, my darling...."

And just at the crest, her name came to his lips in an agony of need. "Casey," he groaned, slipping over into ecstacy. "Oh, Casey. My God, how I love you."

She lay staring up at the ceiling, totally at peace, her hand on Matt's shoulder. Then she shifted onto her side and ran her hand through the wiry hairs of his chest.

"When I was a young girl," she said softly, "I used to dream that love was everything in the world. I was going out with Andy in high school and I was crazy about him and all we wanted was to get married." A gentle smile curved her lips in remembrance. "And we did get married, and pretty soon there were bills to pay and dishes to wash and cars to fix, and love wasn't all I'd thought it was going to be. But Andy and I did love each other and we were happy. And then he got killed...."

Matt pulled her tighter against him as she paused, trying to think of how to say what she must say. "And then I was truly alone, for the first time in my life. Dad had died when I was still in school, and Mom had died soon after I married Andy, and then Andy died. It was horrible. I felt alone, lost, without moorings. And for a while I coped by believing that love wasn't wonderful at all. That when you loved someone, all you got was hurt. And so I started my business and threw myself into it. A couple years later, I woke up one day and realized that the pain was all gone. I was a new woman. A real woman, capable of taking care of myself, not dependent on anyone for anything. And that felt good, really good. I wasn't frightened anymore, and I guess I thought I had everything in the world."

One of Matt's hands slowly stroked her back as she caressed the warm, male chest, pressing her lips into the curve of Matt's shoulder. "And then I met you, and it was like suddenly seeing the sunshine after years of clouds. I had forgotten what it was like to be with a man who lit up your life, who made your heart pound." She closed her eyes and rubbed her cheek against his chest, feeling his arm strong around her. "I'd forgotten what it's *like*, Matt," she whispered, her voice trembling with emotion. "How beautiful it is. What a magical gift it is—like a gift from the gods. And it's strange, but somehow, having been married once and having lost my husband, having lost everything in the world that I had ever wanted and having to start all over again, from the bottom up, now, *this* time it's incredibly more beautiful than it was the first time."

She rose up on one elbow and gazed imploringly into his eyes, willing him to understand, to see the depth of her emotion. "It's like I went blind and suddenly can see again. It's as if I'd been to see a doctor and he told me I was going to die and I went home and believed I was dying, but then he called me up the next day and said, 'Oh, Mrs. Adams, I made a mistake—it's not *you* who's going to die, it's poor Mrs. So-And-So. . . .'"

She sat up, pulling the sheet around her, and pressed her hands together in an attitude of prayer, touching her fingertips to her lips. "Can you see, Matt? Can you understand what you mean to me?" She gazed down into his warm gray eyes and felt her own love burst inside her like fireworks. "You've made me come alive again, Matt."

And he reached up, his smile as tender as any she had ever seen, and drew her back into his arms. "Ah, Casey Adams," he murmured softly. "What a hell of a woman you are. Remind me to have a serious talk with you someday, hmmm?"

Joy and laughter and warmth filled her. "A serious talk," she repeated, grinning at him as she traced his lips with her finger. "Okay, someday I'll remind you to have a serious talk with me. But right now, Mr. Stoner, I'm only interested in one thing."

Sighing exaggeratedly, Matt turned her onto her back and rose up on an elbow. "Women," he said in mock disparagement. "All you ever think about is sex."

13

THE FOLLOWING MORNING Casey floated across the dew-whitened grass, her face radiant, her step buoyant. As she opened the kitchen door, she was humming. Mary O'Reilly turned around, took one look at her, and raised an eyebrow.

"Harrumpphh," Mary said irritably. "It's good to see *someone* in a good mood around here!"

Casey paused before taking off her sweater. "Oh? Who else isn't in a good mood?" she asked, gently teasing. "Besides you?"

"Well," Mary started off, obviously glad to be able to unload her irritations, "Mr. Stoner came in all smiles, and everything was going just fine until that Miss Tyrone appeared." Mary shook a slotted spoon at Casey. "She'd be

145

better off being called Miss Tyrant, if you ask me." Mary tossed her iron-gray head and sniffed. "Of course, no one ever asks me anyway, so I don't know why I bother to comment."

Casey hung her sweater on the back of her chair and bit at her lip. How to handle this? With gentle teasing or taking it more seriously? She decided that Mary needed to be taken seriously. That was probably half the problem between Mary and Pamela Tyrone. Pamela never bothered to give Mary the respect she deserved for doing the job she did so well.

"What happened, Mary?" Casey cocked her head inquiringly, her expression concerned.

"That little bi—" Mary bit off her statement and took a calming breath. "That little whippersnapper *ordered* me to *order* you to bring her breakfast in Mr. Stoner's study at seven thirty sharp. Sharp, mind you! Can you beat that? *Her* ordering *you?*" Mary's face took on a knowing, confiding look. "And I think I know why she's being so bitchy this morning."

"Oh? Why is that?"

"Because Mr. Stoner was whistling."

Casey put a finger to her lips consideringly, not able to follow Mary's logic. "Because Mr. Stoner was whistling," she repeated lamely.

"That's right. Mr. Stoner never whistles."

Casey raised her eyebrows and cocked her head to one side as if perplexed. "He was whistling, but he never whistles, is that what you said?"

"Exactly." Mary put the slotted spoon down and wiped her hands on her apron, clearly pleased with her ability to see situations in perspective.

Casey laughed against her will, shaking her head ruefully. "Mary, you lost me. You just plain lost me."

Mary leaned forward aggressively, like a schoolteacher with a slow learner. "He never whistles, but he was whistling this morning. And who was he with last night? Pamela Nose-In-The-Air Tyrone? No. Casey Adams, that's who. So now we've got a Pamela Nose-Out-Of-Joint Tyrone, and we're all going to suffer."

Casey felt herself flush at Mary's blunt statement, then shook her head in deep perplexity. "I still don't follow you, Mary."

"Well it's as plain as the nose on your face, Casey Adams! Pamela Tyrone is jealous that Mr. Stoner is spending his time with you and enjoying it. He *used* to spend his time with her, working late over those darned reports she kept telling him needed to be written. She's just plain jealous!"

Casey stared down at the floor, mulling over what Mary had just said. Could she be right? That would go a long way in explaining Pamela's behavior toward Casey. Or was Mary just venting her frustrations about Pamela and not really on target at all?

As she tried to sort things out, Casey went about preparing the toast and cup of tea that Pamela always liked in the morning. When she had the tray arranged, she carried it to Matt's study. Knocking softly, she opened the door and went in.

Matt and Pam were at his desk, deeply immersed in a pile of papers. But on seeing Casey, Matt's face lit up with pleasure.

"Good morning, Mrs. Adams." His voice sounded cool and amused, filled with secrets.

"Good morning, Mr. Stoner," she replied, unable to keep a dimple from appearing in her cheek. She shifted her gaze to Pamela. "Here's the breakfast you wanted, Pamela."

Pamela's eyes drifted down Casey's figure, taking in the white slacks and navy-blue T-shirt. Pamela was wearing a lime-green linen dress, her pearls, and expensive leather pumps. She looked the epitome of the rich society woman. "Thank you, Mrs. Adams, you can just leave it over there." Cool disdain dripped from her voice.

Casey chose to ignore it, placing the tray carefully on a small table near a window.

"Taking one of your little trips around the Cape today, Mrs. Adams?" Pam asked sarcastically.

Casey paused, then turned slowly. "Why, no, I hadn't planned on it. Why?"

"No reason. I was just wondering." Her eyes seemed to bore into Casey's, the message unclear but somehow threatening.

Casey turned on her heel, making her way to the door. "Enjoy your breakfast, Miss Tyrone," she said coolly, and then, more warmly, to Matt, "Have a nice morning."

If Matt had noticed anything strange about the interchange, he didn't seem to show it. His head was already bent over his papers. He grunted at Casey and turned to Pamela before Casey was at the door. As she looked back to close the door behind her, Casey saw Pamela pull up a chair next to Matt and place a slim hand on his arm. There was something so possessive about the gesture that Casey stood in the doorway a moment and watched.

Pamela was saying something to him in a very low voice, her expression urgent and troubled. Matt was staring at her, completely absorbed in what she was saying. Casey felt a strange pang go through her. Was this the way they acted together when they were alone? So totally absorbed in each other that another person could remain unobserved?

Closing the door quietly, Casey stood in the hall for a moment. What was Pamela saying that was so important? And what kind of relationship did she have with Matt that gave her the freedom to stroke his arm so caressingly?

A worm of doubt twisted in Casey's midsection, and she spun away and hurried down the hall. What was the matter with her anyway? She had just spent the evening before with Matt, who had finally told her he loved her, and here she was acting jealous over his relationship with his secretary! How foolish of her! Better to spend her time constructively, planning the menu for the cocktail party that would be held Saturday evening.

Within ten seconds all thoughts of Pamela Tyrone were banished. But two hours later, as Casey was putting the final touches on a flower arrangement for the dining table, Pamela appeared in the doorway. When she saw Pamela, Casey wondered how long she had been standing there, watching her.

Casey managed a smile. "Hello. Did you want to see me?"

Pamela closed the door behind her and advanced toward the table. Reaching out with a long, red-glazed fingernail, she stroked a tulip petal. "There's something I think you should know, Casey."

Casey felt an alarm bell go off in her head, shrilling all the way down her spine, ending in a jolt at her feet. Something was coming, but she didn't know what. She summoned her courage and raised calm eyes to Pamela.

"Oh? What is that?"

Pamela appeared to hesitate. "This isn't easy, Casey...."

Irritation at the other woman flared in Casey. "Life isn't easy, Pamela. Do go on."

"All right, let's just say I'm going to give you a little friendly warning."

Casey could barely suppress a hoot of laughter. *Friendly* warning? From *Pamela?* "Oh? And what is that?"

"Simply this. Matt's always got one woman or another falling for him. Last month it was poor little Crystal Fensterwick. This month it's you. Who knows who it will be next month."

"You, perhaps?" Casey asked ironically.

Pam smiled dryly. "No, I fell for him the first month I started working for him. It took a while to get over the hurt. I thought I'd spare you the pain."

"How thoughtful of you."

"You don't believe me? You think I have an ulterior motive."

"Well, now that you mention it...."

Pamela sniffed disdainfully. "All right, then, go ahead and make a fool of yourself."

"I'm not in the habit of making a fool of myself, Pamela, but thank you for your concern. I'll certainly keep it in mind."

"You think he loves you, don't you?" Pamela asked, her voice filled with wonder, as if Casey were a bigger fool than Pam had originally suspected.

Something warned Casey not to say anything. She smiled mysteriously and inserted a daffodil into the flower arrangement. "I work for Mr. Stoner, Pamela. I'm not at liberty to discuss my feelings for him."

"Your feelings were written all over your face this morning!" Pamela snapped.

"Were they?" Casey rearranged a piece of fern and shrugged. "And what feelings were written on Matt's face this morning?"

"Oh God, you poor fool. You *do* think he's in love with you."

Casey felt fear twist in her stomach, but she refused to show it. Smiling serenely, she placed the arrangement carefully in the center of the table. "Spare me your concern, Pamela. I'm afraid I don't need it."

Pamela shrugged elaborately and sauntered toward the door. "Okay, Casey, have it your way. Dream on. But if you think for even one minute that Matt Stoner would really fall in love with you, you're crazy. You're *beneath* him. Face it, Casey. He needs someone from his own world, a woman from a wealthy family, someone who knows his world and is comfortable in it. Don't be a fool, Casey Adams. You wouldn't last in his world for a month." With that, Pamela whirled on her spike heel and slammed the door behind her.

Casey stared at the door, then put a hand to her stomach. Suddenly she felt very weak. Very ill. She had to get out. She needed some air. Some time to think. Yes, she must get away from here, from everything about this horrible, horrible place.

Rushing from the room, Casey didn't even see the look of concern on Mary O'Reilly's face as she ran through the kitchen and slammed the door behind her. She was too intent on her own pain. What if Pamela Tyrone were right? Oh, dear God, what if she were right. . . .

Casey drove blindly at first, letting instinct guide her small car. She was almost to Hyannis before she thought of where she was going. By then she knew—to the great, undulating expanse of dunes outside Provincetown, at the extreme tip of the Cape. The weather that had seemed so promising early that morning had turned threatening. The sky was leaden, with dark clouds scudding low on the horizon. A brisk wind battered the small car, forcing Casey to grip the steering wheel tightly to keep on the right side of the road.

"It just matches my mood," she muttered out loud, scanning the lowering sky.

Just outside Provincetown she pulled her car to a stop on the side of the road. The scrubby pines of Cape Cod had long ago given way to sweeping expanses of rolling dunes. Thick thatches of dune grass were almost flat from the wind, and a stinging spray of sand blew in gusts against the car's windshield. Ignoring the rolling black clouds, Casey turned off the ignition and got out.

The wind hit her with stunning force, blowing back her hair and flattening her clothes against her body. Reaching into the back seat of the car, she pulled out a yellow oilcloth slicker and threw it around her. With it billowing out behind her like a yellow sail, she proceeded to climb the dunes, toward the ocean.

Bowing her head against the force of the wind, she made her way up the dune to its crest, then her breath caught in her throat. The force of the wind was so much stronger here that for a moment she thought she might be plucked up and whirled into the sky, a yellow-caped dot in all that seething blackness. Ahead of her the ocean raged, a seething, crashing wall of angry water. Whitecapped waves massed far out from shore, gathering in speed and size as they neared their destination. Finally, in a frenzy of splintering fury, they dashed against the shore, dragging the unwilling sand back into the ocean, as if not content to wreak their havoc on the shore alone.

Casey stood at the top of the dunes, at once both frightened and exhilarated. She felt alone in all the world, outlined against the raging sky, confronted by the seething ocean.

Not a soul anywhere. No one else had wandered out. The boats were safe at anchor in their harbors. She stood alone, huddled in the oilcloth slicker, and stared at the sea.

It was like looking into her own soul. All the torrential storminess of the ocean was inside herself. She was torn by doubts, ripped by fear, in love with a man, yet afraid of his world. *Why* hadn't she ever seen it before? Why had she hidden it from herself? She wasn't afraid that Matt would think she didn't fit into his wealthy, high-society world. She was more afraid that he would be right, that despite her successful business, her expensive clothes, and polite manners, which disguised her lower-class upbringing, despite all she had achieved, she would never fit in. Faced with the prospect of joining the ranks of the wealthy, on their terms, her confidence was shattered.

Casey lifted her chin defiantly. Well, no, not *shattered* . . . not really. Just in disarray. She was afraid, she had to admit that. "You're from South Boston," that terrible inner voice told her, "not Beacon Hill. Silly girl, how would you ever fit in?"

Groaning inwardly, Casey turned and ran down the dune toward the shelter of her car. What was she going to do? How could she ever be comfortable in Matt's world? And how could she for one moment believe he would ever want to marry her? He might have fallen in love with her, but marry her? After declaring his love for her, he had said he would have to have a serious talk with her one day, and she, foolish girl, had thought he meant to ask her to marry him. What if, instead, he knew he must tell her that she wasn't good enough to be his wife, entertain his wealthy guests, bear his children?

Slamming the car door behind her, Casey slumped in the seat. The wind hammered on the car, like the voices of doubt that hammered in her ears. Putting her hands up, she pressed them against her ears as if to ward off the noise and confusion. She sat that way, unthinking, eyes closed, for what could have been a half an hour, then she raised her head and saw that the storm had broken. Rain beat down in steady harmony on the car, almost soothing after the pre-storm intensity. Slowly, watching the rain sweep out of the gray skies, listening to its steady drumming on the roof of the car, Casey felt peace return. She didn't know how she would resolve this dilemma, but she knew that she would. She had been afraid when Andy died, but she had found the strength to go on, to start a business, to make it a success. And while she might be afraid now, that didn't mean that she couldn't face her fear and conquer it. A slow, impish grin broke over her features. Pamela Tyrone and her dire warnings be damned. If Matt Stoner loved Casey enough to want to marry her, then she would fit into his genteel world. She'd take it by storm. She would not, she vowed, become *like* them, but rather live *with* them, as just herself, just plain old Casey Adams, the little Irish girl from Southie who had made good.

Dinner was just being served when she finally arrived back at Matt's house in Woods Hole. She had dawdled in the shops in Provincetown, shopping for gifts for Joanie and a few other close friends back home in Boston. Her earlier fears had lifted, leaving her feeling free and light-hearted. Slipping into her seat opposite Matt, she flicked open her napkin, spread it on her lap, and lifted sparkling eyes to his. But the eyes that met hers were as gray as the stormy sea at Provincetown. Puzzled, Casey cocked her head questioningly. What was the matter? Why did he appear to be so angry with her? But there was no way to get those questions answered, for Pamela Tyrone seemed inordinately interested in engaging her in conversation.

"So you did drive around the Cape, after all, Casey," she was saying, sounding her usual arch self.

Casey turned to her. "Yes, I decided I wanted to get out for a while."

"Not the most pleasant day for a drive, I'd think," Pamela said, balancing three peas on her sterling-silver fork with beautiful precision. "Unless, of course, you met some friends."

Casey felt a vague stirring of alarm, but she didn't know why. She put it down to her general distrust of Pamela and shrugged carelessly. "I didn't meet anyone. I poked around the shops in Provincetown for a while, bought a couple of gifts. You know. Just lazed the day away."

"Provincetown?" Pamela repeated. "Why, isn't that where that Alonzo Davis has his yacht moored?" Her blue eyes traveled toward Anna. "Weren't you saying he was seen in Provincetown the other day?"

Anna nodded. "That's what I read in the paper." She grinned at Casey. "So did you have that talk with Davis, when you ran into him at Provincetown, like you said you would, Casey?"

Casey felt all eyes on her and, worse, felt embarrassed color slowly seeping up from her neck into her face. What was the matter with her? Why was she acting guilty when she wasn't? "Talk?" she asked, knowing she sounded too innocent. "What talk?"

Anna was looking somewhat puzzled. "Don't you remember? You joked with Stefanos yesterday about having a talk with Davis when you ran into him on your jaunts around the Cape." Anna shrugged apologetically. "It was only a joke, Casey."

Casey forced a laugh and stole a quick look at Matt. "Oh, yes, now I remember. No, I'm afraid I didn't run into Mr. Davis. Next time, perhaps."

Anna smiled vaguely and launched into a discussion about the latest Hollywood star to get married, but Casey barely listened. On one side of her, Pamela Tyrone sat eyeing her with cunning deliberation. Across from her, Matt looked like a thundercloud. Only Stefanos seemed interested in Anna's chatter. Sighing, Casey picked at her food and wondered why she felt so uncomfortable. Was it all in her head, or was there something going on here that she didn't understand?

Dinner couldn't end fast enough for Casey. The only thing that made it bearable was that Anna kept up a steady stream of innocuous chatter, covering up the fact that Matt ate sullenly, his eyes on his plate, and Pamela seemed lost in her own glacial world. For her own part, Casey wanted to squirm in her seat like a child waiting for recess. She resisted, but silently counted the minutes until dessert was served, coffee poured, and she could politely excuse herself.

"Going to bed so early, Casey?" Pamela asked.

The very tone of voice set Casey's teeth on edge. She forced a smile even though she felt like screaming. "Yes, I'm rather tired. It was a long day."

Matt stood up so abruptly that his chair almost fell over backward. Catching it, he sat it firmly in place and gave Casey a stoney-faced look. "I'll escort you home."

His words brought her no pleasure. She merely nodded and turned from the room. Once out on the terrace, she crossed her arms and hugged herself against the chill in the air. "You seem rather miffed, Matt," she said quietly. "Is something wrong? Aren't your talks with Stefanos going well?"

"Why would *you* want to know?" he asked coldly.

Both hurt and puzzled by his tone of voice, she turned troubled eyes to him. "Why wouldn't I want to know? I'm interested in you and your work. I want to share it with you. We've talked in the past, you've confided in me. Why can't you now? Are things so very confidential now?"

Matt's face looked like granite. "Such admirable sentiments, Casey, my dear."

Casey felt as if a knife had plunged into her heart. Why was he so horribly sarcastic? "Matt..." She stopped and lay a slim hand on his arm. "Matt, what *is* it?"

He seemed to be struggling with himself, his face looking like a battlefield, then he took a deep breath and ran a hand through his hair. "Things *are* at a delicate point in our negotiations, Casey. I think it's better if I don't talk to anyone about them." He stood gazing out toward the harbor, the wind whipping his shaggy hair back from his face. He seemed so remote from her, so cold, that Casey wanted to bury herself in his arms, to wrap herself around him and plead for him to come back to her, to be the man who had held her last night and told her he loved her. What could she do to get that man back? Or should she even try? She didn't know Matt well enough yet. She might need years and years to know how to handle his various moods. Perhaps it was best to remain quiet and let him brood over his problems alone. But was that how she wanted to spend her time with him? A mere playmate while he hassled with business? She wanted to share his problems, to help him cope. . . .

Sighing, she bit at her lip and began walking once more, heading for her cottage. For a moment, she thought Matt wasn't going to follow, then she heard his hurried step and felt his hard hand on her arm as he swung her around to face him. His face seemed savage in the dim light from the cottage lantern.

"Don't ever leave me like that, Casey," he snarled. "Do you hear me?"

The pressure of his hand on her arm was painful, yet his words hurt her even more. Bewildered, she could only search his stormy eyes. "Matt, what are you *talking* about?"

He stared down at her, looking torn in two by some terrible conflict, then he groaned and pulled her into his arms. His mouth crushed hers as his arms pinned her to the steel frame of his body. She felt ravaged, but something in her responded to his primitive force, opening to meet his driving need.

"God, Casey," he groaned. "Don't ever leave me and don't ever lie to me. Promise me that."

"Matt." She pulled away, completely confused by his words. "Darling, I'm not going to leave you. Or lie to you. Ever."

His hands gripped her upper arms. "What do you do on those drives you take around the Cape, Casey?"

Startled, she could only laugh. "Why, nothing. I shop. I sit and look at the ocean." She shrugged. "Nothing, really— just relax, I guess."

"You're not meeting another man?"

Stunned, she stared up at him. "Another man?" She

searched and searched for the reason for his question. What could she have ever said or done to make him suddenly suspect that she was seeing another man? "Matt, darling, *no.*"

He seemed to weigh her answer, then, with a husky sigh, pulled her once more into his arms. "Casey," he murmured, running his hands up and down her back. "It's all right, then. Everything's all right."

"Yes," she whispered, clinging to him, her eyes closed in desperate fear. "Yes," she repeated, over and over again, while deep inside the insidious fear grew. It wasn't all right. Something was terribly, terribly wrong.

14

THE COCKTAIL PARTY was in full swing. Bursts of laughter punctuated the buzz of conversation in the crowded living room. The soft melody of a Gershwin tune being played on the piano in the corner of the room was almost lost amid the milling mass of bodies and the tinkle of ice in expensive glasses. Over everything lay a cloud of cigarette smoke, wreathing the heads of the guests.

Casey stood unobtrusively to one side, scanning the room. She spied Dorothea and Herman Fensterwick, who had arrived at Woods Hole from their summer home in Chatham. Their daughter Crystal and her new boyfriend were gazing at each other adoringly on a couch off to the side of the room. Casey smiled, remembering her fears that Matt had been romantically interested in Crystal. She saw now how completely unfounded those fears had been. Crystal had kissed Matt resoundingly on the cheek upon arrival, then turned rapturous eyes to the young blond man at her side.

"Steve Dalton," she had breathed. "Meet Matt Stoner and Casey Adams. I had a terrible crush on Matt a while back, but luckily he had the good sense to point me in *your* direction!"

Steve blushed and glowed at Crystal, who had glowed back at him, while Matt had watched with avuncular amusement and Casey had wanted to reach out and hug him for being the wonderful man she now realized he was. How foolish all her fears had been. He was no womanizer, no international playboy. He *was* a wealthy man, of course, and Casey still had that problem to resolve, not to mention that terrible jealous strain that seemed to have seeped into Matt recently. She frowned thoughtfully, but pushed her thoughts away. There was no time now to dwell on Matt's recent accusations that she was seeing another man behind his back. She had more pressing matters to attend to. Since arriving at the Cape, she had gradually assumed the role of hostess for Matt, so that now, while she planned the menus and decorations, she let Mary and two hired girls prepare everything.

Smiling at a group of guests, Casey began to circulate once more. With her trained eye, it was easy for her to mingle with the guests, signaling a waitress to empty an overflowing ashtray here, refresh a drink there, or pass a tray laden with puff-pastry hors d'oeuvres.

Pausing near the French doors, Casey searched the room for Matt. She found him standing in the opposite corner with Stefanos and James Fenton, an assistant secretary in the Department of Commerce. Fenton was the main reason for this party, and Casey sighed with relief, realizing that so far everything was a success. The food was being devoured hungrily, the drinks were overflowing, the guests were all laughing and chatting happily, and, best of all, Stefanos and James Fenton were laughing boisterously, watched amiably by Matt.

Casey walked toward the trio, smiling and nodding at the clusters of guests, reaching out here to take someone's hand or there to pat an arm in a friendly gesture. She had a natural flair for hostessing, something she had always suspected but had sublimated by being the brains behind the scene—planning the food, creating the decorations, and helping other women put on perfect parties. Now she was finding that she liked being in the thick of the action. It was fun mingling with the guests and actually seeing their enjoyment, so much better than doing all the work and then disappearing to let some other woman enjoy the results.

For the first time, Casey's fears that she wouldn't fit into the actual social life in Matt's wealthy world were beginning to evaporate. Here was actual proof that she could do it, and do it faultlessly. Perhaps Pamela Tyrone's dire warnings had merely been prompted by jealousy, and a desire to drive Casey away. For faced with the actual test of fitting in, Casey was doing quite nicely, thank you.

Smiling, she advanced on the trio of men in the corner. "Why is it that all the most interesting and handsome men are hiding in this corner when there are so many beautiful women just aching to meet and talk with you?" she asked laughingly.

Stefanos's black eyes gleamed. "I keep in the corner so Anna can shine," he explained. "If I flirt with other women, she hits me when we're alone in our room." He shrugged helplessly, laughing out loud at the image of so large and dominating a man cowering before the petite Anna Copeland.

James Fenton smiled with the practiced charm of a lifetime government diplomat. "I must say, Mrs. Adams, you have the knack for getting people to enjoy themselves. I can't remember when I've had such a good time. Those parties in Washington could use a little of your brand of hostessing."

Casey glowed, aware that Matt was also beaming with pride. She took James Fenton's hand. "Come with me, James," she said, leading him toward a group of men and women who were congregated near the bar. "Give these amateur politicians the benefit of an insider's knowledge. And don't be modest. Tell them about the major part you played in our government's negotiations in South America last year."

Fenton stared at Casey in surprise. "How did you know about that?"

"I make it a point of knowing all about my guests," she grinned, then left him to drift among the guests. From out of nowhere Matt materialized at her side.

"You give one mean party, Mrs. Adams," he said, smiling down at her.

Casey felt elation surge through her, as well as a sense of relief. These past few days she had never been sure how Matt was going to act—whether he would be kind and loving, or accusatory, claiming that she was seeing another man when she drove around the Cape. Tonight, he seemed to have forgotten his recent suspicions and was the old Matt, looking at her with loving gray eyes, eyes that promised happiness that could last forever.

"After next Saturday's dinner party," he was saying, "I want you all to myself. Do you realize that the entire month of May has almost gone by and we've hardly been alone?"

She nodded ironically, raising an eyebrow comically. "I realize all too well. I'll be looking forward to that. I don't get to see you enough for my liking at all."

From her elbow, a female voice intruded. "Is that why you escape to other parts of the Cape, Casey? To find *other* male companionship?"

A chill descended on Casey. She turned to find Pamela Tyrone eyeing her coolly. Casey's eyes skittered toward Matt, and she realized he had stiffened at Pamela's words. Casey felt icy anger invade her veins. How dare Pamela Tyrone insinuate such a thing? Was *she* the source of Matt's recent jealousy? Unconsciously, Casey straightened her already regal posture. Keeping her chin up, she regarded Pam with a serene expression on her face.

"No, Pam," she said smoothly, "I go to other parts of the Cape only because they're so much nicer without you there." With that, she turned and walked gracefully away, her back straight and proud, her head tilted at a dignified angle.

The picture of ease on the outside, inwardly Casey was shaking. Gradually she made her way through the crowd, toward the hall, intent on getting away to the relative quiet of the kitchen. There she could pretend she was checking on the food, while in reality she would be repairing her shattered composure.

She had only a few minutes of peace in the familiar surroundings of the kitchen before Pamela caught up with her. "Oh, Casey, Matt asked me to give you a message."

Casey wanted to ignore the vicious voice, but she knew she couldn't. What message had Matt entrusted to Pam for her? She had to know, even though she dreaded to hear it. "Yes?" she asked quietly. "And what is it, Miss Tyrone?"

Pamela smiled cruelly. "Only that he won't be seeing you tonight after the party after all. He and Stefanos and James Fenton are all flying to Washington on an early flight tomorrow morning. He said he'd see you next Saturday evening, at the dinner party."

Casey felt as if a fist had clutched at her heart. She had been looking forward to being alone with Matt. He had promised her.... Hiding her disappointment, she nodded to Pamela and turned to leave, only to have Pamela put a cool hand on her arm to detain her.

"You see, Casey, it's happening already, isn't it?" she asked.

"Happening already?" Casey asked. "I don't know what you mean."

"Matt's beginning to realize you're not the woman for him and never could be. He's beginning to want to get out of his latest entanglement. I warned you, Casey, but you wouldn't listen, would you? Oh, no, you were determined that he was really in love with you." Pamela's eyes laughed scornfully. "He always uses this tactic, Casey, in case you're wondering. He tires of his latest girlfriend and starts accusing her of being unfaithful. It's the perfect excuse to drop her when another, more suitable or more desirable, woman comes along."

"And you're helping him, aren't you, Pam?" Casey asked. "That little comment about finding other male companionship was just calculated to aid him in his cause, wasn't it?"

Pamela laughed musically. "Why, Casey, what an absurd idea!" She waved a slim hand and turned to go. "If the shoe fits wear it, I always say."

"But in this case, Pamela, the shoe *doesn't* fit. You're consciously trying to cram it on my foot. But it won't work."

Pamela turned back, looking completely at ease. "Won't it? I wouldn't be too sure, Casey. I wouldn't be too sure at all."

That night Casey lay in bed tossing and turning. Could Pamela Tyrone's explanation of Matt's puzzling behavior be correct? Did he tire of his latest lover and turn her off by becoming jealous over a nonexistent rival? It seemed uttlerly preposterous, but what other explanation was there? Matt had never exhibited the slightest signs of jealousy in the past, but ever since her return from Provincetown about two weeks ago, he had been mysteriously moody, alternating between barely suppressed anger and agonized apologies for doubting her.

Lying in bed, listening to the muted murmur of the sea, Casey thought of Matt, of all that she knew of him, and came to the conclusion that something else lay behind his behavior. But what? The only explanation she could come up with was the one she feared the most—that he had found her lacking somehow and wanted to stop seeing her. But hadn't the party tonight been a huge success? Hadn't it been due to her? Hadn't she fit in and been warmly received as the hostess, even by her old nemesis Dorothea Fensterwick?

If only she could go to him, if only she could sneak out into the chill night air, up to the main house, to his room, and talk to him. But something held her back, something that she had never quite come to terms with. It had to do with the fear that while he could come down here to visit her late into the night, he wouldn't want her to come to his room. What would the other guests think, after all, if Matthew Charles Stoner were found to be conducting an affair with his caterer?

Bitter tears washed down Casey's face. She told herself that she was being a fool, that of course he didn't feel that way, that those were the sentiments of the eighteenth century, not of today's civilization, but nevertheless, the cruel doubts shook her, keeping her awake far into the night. The first fingers of dawn were stirring before she finally fell into a troubled sleep.

Casey had taken special pains for the following Saturday evening's dinner party. It would be a formal meal, but not too elaborate, starting off with consommé, then a lobster soufflé, followed by rack of lamb served with potatoes Anna and fresh asparagus. A green salad with avocado and lemon dressing would follow the main course, topped off by raspberry mousse.

Dressed in a kelly-green chiffon floor-length dress, Casey made a final inspection of the dining room before joining the others in the living room for pre-dinner cocktails. She felt nervous flutters attack her usually calm stomach. She hadn't seen Matt since the week before, when Pamela Tryone's comment had turned him into granite. All week she had fretted over his behavior, worrying that her relationship with him, which had blossomed into love (he *had* said he loved her, hadn't he?) was now souring. By the next weekend, her stay at the Cape would be over and she would be returning home. A couple of weeks ago, she had thought she might be returning to the possibility of life with Matt, as his wife. Now, she wasn't sure where she stood.

Peering into a mirror, she checked her appearance one final time, then took a deep breath and walked toward the living room. Instinct told her that his first look at her would reveal the truth of how he felt. It would be in his gray eyes, either love or . . . Casey's thoughts veered away from any other possibility. She couldn't face any other, but knew now that she must enter the room, must face him, must face the realities that lay ahead, whatever they might be.

She hesitated on the threshold, scanning the room quickly until she found Matt. He was standing near the fireplace holding a drink while talking to Stefanos and Anna. At the far end of the room, Pamela Tyrone and her escort for the evening were talking with James and Miriam Fenton. There were no other guests. It was to be a small, intimate dinner. If all went well, tomorrow Matt and Stefanos would finalize their negotiations and sign a multiyear contract.

At that moment Stefanos noticed Casey standing in the doorway and grinned at her, causing Matt to turn toward her. If there had been the crash of cymbals or soaring of violins, Casey wouldn't have felt more wonderful. His eyes were warm, smoky gray, gazing at her with all the longing she was feeling herself. Without knowing it, she advanced toward him, her face radiant, her eyes glowing. No one else existed. Furniture melted out of her way, the walls receded. There was nothing, there was no one, but Matt.

And then she was in front of him and he was taking her hand, bending to touch her cheek gently with his lips. His voice, like warm velvet, stroked her senses. "I've missed you, Casey Adams. I've missed you like the very devil."

She had never felt more alive in her life. Tilting her head up, she let all the love she felt glow in her eyes. "Oh, I've missed you too, Matt," she whispered.

There were a few more seconds of total isolation, of each wrapped up in the other, then the room and its occupants intervened. Stefanos roared a greeting, Anna made a witty remark, and the Fentons crossed the room to greet her. Suddenly Casey was smothered in hostessing duties, Matt necessarily forgotten. Aglow with happiness, Casey turned to include Pam and her escort in the conversation and felt herself come down to earth with a thud.

Dressed in a brilliant red gown, Pamela was especially beautiful tonight, looking like a wild orchid in a room full of geraniums. Her color was abnormally high and her eyes glittered as if she had a fever. Staring at her, Casey realized that what she was seeing were tears, unshed tears, shimmering in the icy depths. Before Casey could speak to her, Pamela turned on her heel and left the room.

Casey stood and stared after the other woman, feeling a sudden rush of insight. The tears, the hectic circles of red in her cheeks—they had been the result of Pamela keeping a powerful rein on overpowering emotion. It struck Casey then that Pamela loved Matt with perhaps the same urgency that she herself loved him. It was killing Pamela to stand by and see the man she loved fall in love with another woman.

Turning away, Casey felt a curious depression settle over her. How strange that she should feel this compassion for a woman who seemed to wish her nothing but harm. But then she realized why she did feel it. It might have been she, Casey Adams, watching Matt fall in love with Pamela, rather than the other way around. And with swift comprehension Casey realized it was easy to feel compassion when everything in one's life was going as one wanted it to go. She thought perhaps her emotions would be vastly different if Matt and she hadn't fallen in love.

Casey had no further time for speculation, for Mary O'Reilly appeared in the doorway to announce that dinner was ready. The guests went into the dining room, and there was the usual pleasant commotion as everyone settled into their places. At the last moment, Pamela appeared and slipped into her seat.

"Ah," said Stefanos. "Another perfect meal, I hope."

Casey smiled broadly. "I hope you enjoy it. I've tried to go to special pains to make it as perfect as possible."

The bowls of consommé were set in front of each guest. Because Casey liked to sample everything she served, she spared no time in dipping her spoon into the bowl. At the first sip, she almost gasped.

It was atrocious! Stunned, Casey took another sip and felt her face go white. My God, it was terrible. There was enough salt in it to preserve an entire herd of buffalo. What had happened? When she had left the kitchen to get ready for dinner, everything had been fine. Had someone accidentally spilled a container of salt in it and not known? Or been afraid to confess?

Not wanting to look up, she knew she must. If her consommé tasted like this, everyone's did. Schooling her features to be calm, she raised her eyes and saw her worst fears confirmed. There was a mixture of looks on the faces—shock, embarrassment, even sly amusement.

Casey's eyes darted to Matt and she felt her heart plummet to her feet. He looked positively livid.

So much for fitting into his world, she thought irrelevantly, then knew she must take matters into hand. Standing up, she smiled graciously. "This is terribly embarrassing," she said, her eyes filled with troubled laughter, "but I now realize where I dropped the salt shaker."

For a moment there was complete silence, then a few titters of amusement, followed by the relief of open laughter. Casey felt her heartbeat return to normal. Thank God for a sense of humor, she told herself, and sent an apologetic glance toward Matt. His steely gray eyes had warmed up considerably when he realized that she had salvaged an awkward situation with her humor.

But when the lobster soufflé was placed on the table, Casey felt a tremor go through her. Please let it be all right, she prayed, and hastily sampled it.

It was like the recurrence of a nightmare. It couldn't be happening! Someone had sprinkled salt and white pepper all over the soufflé!

Swallowing with difficulty, Casey pushed her chair back and stood up, feeling unsteady. Once was explainable. Twice was inexcusable.

"I'd advise everyone not to try to soufflé," she said quietly.

Seven faces turned to her inquiringly. She tried to find something to say, some plausible excuse, but her mind was suddenly blank. "I . . . I don't know how to say this, but there's something wrong with the soufflé."

Matt's eyes had grown hard, but he said nothing. Casey wished she could run from the room and bury her head. In five years of catering parties, nothing like this had ever happened to her. If it had, she would still be scrubbing bathrooms. This was too much to handle. How could she possibly explain it? And it was the most important dinner of her entire stay at the Cape, the one meal she had prepared entirely herself.

"This is terribly embarrassing," she said softly, and signaled the two young girls to remove the plates. "It appears we'll have to get right to the main course."

Pamela Tryone's droll voice spoke up: "I hope it isn't *burned.* . . ."

An uneasy silence followed the remark. Casey's face flamed with embarrassed color. Matt drummed on the table, his face as unmoving as granite. Stefanos sat back and folded his arms, showing no emotion. Anna lit a cigarette and puffed on it languidly, as if this were an everyday occurrence in Hollywood. James and Miriam Fenton stared at their wine glasses, perhaps unaccustomed to faux pas in official Washington. Pamela's dinner companion fiddled with his cuff links, looking like he wished he were a thousand miles away. Pamela alone sat smiling serenely. As if to call attention to herself, she reached up and smoothed her dark hair.

"I suppose this is what can be expected from caterers from time to time," she said cattily, and Casey felt the stirrings of anger under her embarrassment.

"It's never happened before," Casey said in a low voice, "but I suppose there's always a first time."

"Especially when the dinner's so important," Pamela answered waspishly.

The undercurrents in the room were charged with electricity. The guests shifted uncomfortably in their chairs, unable to meet each others' eyes. Casey felt a deadly calm come over her. A storm was about to break, the air was ripe with it. All she could hope to do was ride it out gracefully.

And then, from the corner of her eye, Casey caught sight of Mary waving frantically to her from a crack in the doorway. Feeling that she wouldn't be surprised if the kitchen ceiling had fallen in, Casey excused herself.

"I'll just be a moment," she said, smiling graciously. "I suppose I'd better check on things in the kitchen."

"To see if you can do any *more* damage?" Pamela quipped.

Casey's hands curled around the frame of her chair, but

she managed to hold her temper in rein. "If you'll all excuse me," she said quietly, nodding politely, then walked from the room.

Outside the door, Mary O'Reilly was frantic. "My God, my God, something terrible's happened!"

Casey put a comforting hand on Mary's trembling arm. "Something else?" she asked wryly, trying to jostle Mary from her wide-eyed fear. "What is it this time? Did the rack of lamb come back to life? Is the poor dear bleating in the kitchen for its grain?"

Tears welled up in Mary's eyes. "Oh, Mrs. Adams, I don't know how it happened. Honestly I don't, but someone . . . somehow, the stove got turned up to 550 degrees. You know, I was keeping the lamb warm in the oven so it'd be just right when we served it, but . . ." Mary scrubbed at the tears that streamed down her face. "Oh, Mrs. Adams, it's ruined. It's *charred!*"

Casey kneaded her forehead, her eyes closed, trying to figure a way out of this mess. Finally she sighed and patted Mary's arm. "Don't worry a minute longer. Go phone for reservations at a restaurant up in Falmouth. We'll just go out for dinner and chalk it up to gremlins in the kitchen."

Mary dabbed at her eyes. "Honestly," she whispered, her voice trembling. "I don't know how it happened. You know yourself that everything was perfect when you left the kitchen to get dressed. And I swear to you, I never touched that dial on the oven. And as for the soufflé and consommé—" Mary shook her head worriedly back and forth. "I think someone did it intentionally."

Casey stared at Mary, not wanting to believe anyone could stoop to such an action, but realizing that three disasters in a row in one meal was too much of a coincidence. Again she patted Mary's arm. "Just make the reservations, Mary. Our first duty is to entertain our guests and make them as comfortable as possible. I'll go back and inform everyone that dinner will be delayed until we can drive up to Falmouth."

Taking a deep breath, Casey entered the dining room, and was relieved to see that Matt had stepped in graciously as host and had relaxed everyone by telling a series of rambling tales of past fluff-ups. When Casey took her seat, he turned to her with questioning eyes.

"All's well, I trust?" he asked, and Casey saw with a sinking heart that while he appeared friendly and at ease on the surface, there was a definite fury lurking in the back of those granite-gray eyes.

Casey sighed. "I'm afraid not. Gremlins," she explained, smiling ruefully. "In five years of catering, nothing like this has ever happened before. I only pray it doesn't again, or I'll have to go back to scrubbing bathrooms on Beacon Hill."

There was a shocked silence around the table, and Casey grinned at it. There. It hadn't been so bad to admit her background. In fact, it felt rather good. She was herself, and proud of it. If these rich and beautiful people couldn't accept her for what she was, as well as where she had come from, then be damned to them.

"I've asked Mary to call for reservations at a restaurant in Falmouth," she explained. "So perhaps we should all get our wraps and decide whose cars we'll ride in."

Pamela's blue eyes sparkled with frost. "You expect to get out of this that easily?" she demanded. "You did it deliberately and you know it! It's all been a malicious plan from the very start. I knew there was something going on from the moment I saw you in that restaurant in Boston with Alonzo Davis!"

Stunned, Casey stared at Pamela Tyrone. What in heaven's name could she possibly mean? She glanced at Matt and saw that his tanned face had paled. His lips were sealed in a tight line, his hand knotted into a fist, his knuckles white from tension.

"Pam," he said, his voice like a whiplash, "I think we'd best launder our dirty linen in private." He looked past his secretary toward Stefanos. "Would you mind very much if you and Anna took the Fentons to dinner without us tonight?"

Stefanos shrugged, his face suggesting that anything was fine with him. Only his sharp black eyes suggested that he was keenly interested in what was going on. He darted a suspicious look at Casey that made her want to crawl under the table. She resisted, but just barely, by taking a deep breath to steady herself.

Matt turned to Ken Turner, Pamela's dinner date. "Ken, we're sorry this has happened. You're welcome to go with Stefanos and the others if you like."

Ken stood up so fast his chair almost fell over.

"Er . . . well, uh . . . no, I think not. Pressing business," he muttered, his face burning with embarrassment. "Really have to go. . . ." He turned and almost ran from the room, providing the only comic relief Casey figured she was likely to see the rest of the evening.

Matt looked around the table. "It's settled then. Stefanos and Anna and the Fentons will, we hope, enjoy a disaster-free meal in Falmouth while we here mop up in the kitchen." His steel-gray eyes swept from Pamela to Casey. "Ladies, shall we adjourn to the study?"

Pamela tossed her elegant head, as if she were quite ready to tell all she knew. Casey merely studied Matt with sad eyes. Could he possibly believe she would have done this on purpose? She *loved* him. She wanted only to help him, not hurt him. Couldn't he see that? Sighing, she nodded and stood up.

"To the study," she said, making an effort to sound valiant. "To our various fates. . . ."

15

"AND SO YOU believe Casey deliberately spoiled tonight's dinner so that Stefanos and I wouldn't sign that agreement tomorrow, is that correct, Pam?" Matt sat with an expressionless face, his eyes a clear, cool gray as he watched his secretary.

"Yes!" The patches of red were vibrant in Pamela's cheeks. "It all fits! Here." She rummaged in her pocketbook and brought out a photograph and thrust it at Matt. "When Kevin and I were doing that layout about the market renovation in Boston, we saw Casey and Alonzo Davis in the restaurant. It just so happened that Kevin took a picture of the two of them." Pamela smiled dryly. "It *is* incriminating."

Casey watched as Matt studied the picture, then handed

it to her noncomittally. Looking down at it, Casey recalled the exact instant when a flashbulb had exploded. It had caught Alonzo in the act of kissing her upturned palm. Pamela was right—it *did* look incriminating. Sighing heavily, Casey handed it back to Matt.

"Do you have anything to say, Casey?" he asked.

Casey shrugged. "He's European, very continental. He was bowing and hand-kissing all over the place. It was purely a business meeting. He had called that morning and requested to meet with me at that particular restaurant. I went, met him, listened to his proposition that I work for him for the month of May at his home in the Bahamas, and refused. I'd already taken the assignment here."

Pamela snorted. "Oh, come now, Casey. Any woman in her right mind wouldn't refuse a month in the Bahamas as opposed to little old Cape Cod. Why not admit that you and Davis are lovers and he was plotting with you to get secrets out of Matt so he could scuttle their business talks."

Casey felt increasingly cold, but refused to drop her professional demeanor. Since this entire horrible episode had begun, she had called upon her natural poise and skills in emergency situations and they had held her up well so far. She wasn't about to abandon them now and get emotional.

"Pamela, do you honestly think that by ruining a meal I could ruin such an important agreement? That's utterly preposterous."

"Is it? Maybe just the realization that there was a spy in the house would be enough to make Stefanos not sign the agreement." Pamela smiled archly as if her defense rested, then turned to Matt. "Matt, I *warned* you when I read that Davis was seen in Provincetown. That was the day Casey went up to Provincetown. And she's been driving all over the Cape since she's gotten here. What more proof do you need? It's as obvious as the nose on her lying face."

Matt sighed heavily and swiveled his chair so that his back was to the women. Casey watched him anxiously, seeing the dejected droop to his usually military posture, feeling her heart twist with fear. What if he believed Pamela over her? What could she do to convince him but state the truth—that she didn't know how the meal had been ruined, that she had only met Alonzo Davis once, but had been afraid to admitting it because for some reason she felt guilty. Saying that would only make her look even more guilty.

Matt picked up the phone and punched the intercom button. "Mary? Will you come in here?" He put the phone down and looked up at the two women. "Perhaps now we'll find out what's been going on."

Mary twisted her hands in her apron, looking both frightened and brave at the same time. Her chin was up, but her eyes were fearful. She sat on the edge of a large chair, shifting uncomfortably.

"That's right, Mr. Stoner. When Mrs. Adams left the kitchen, everything tasted just fine. We both sampled a little of everything. Cooks *always* do," she added with a scornful look at Pamela Tyrone.

"And Mrs. Adams never returned to the kitchen after she left?" Matt asked.

"That's right. She went back to her cottage and got dressed, then I saw her come up the lawn and go through the French doors into the dining room. She likes to check the place settings and flowers, you know. Then she went into the living room. A few minutes later Pamela Tyrone came into the kitchen and told the two girls that Mrs. Adams wanted them to check the dining room. Then she told me that Mrs. Adams wanted me to announce that dinner was ready."

Matt stared at Mary solemnly. "So the only person who was in the kitchen alone besides you or the two servers was Pam?"

Mary stared at the floor thoughtfully, then slowly raised her head. "Yes, sir, I do believe that's right."

Casey felt her heartbeat accelerating. She had never told Pamela to ask Mary to announce dinner. Pamela had left the living room on her own accord, her eyes brimming with unshed tears, her cheeks reflecting the high color of barely restrained emotion. Casey closed her eyes briefly, feeling tiredness wash over her. Had this all been the doing of Pamela Tyrone? And if so, for what possible reason?

Matt smiled at Mary. "All right, Mary. That will be all." Mary bounded out of the chair and made for the door, relief showing all over her face. When the door closed behind her, the room was suddenly quiet. Casey sat and watched Matt, who was looking at his desk, his face inscrutable. Pamela's face had become even more red, and she was smoking a cigarette in short, nervous puffs.

The silence stretched until finally Pamela mashed out her cigarette and uncrossed her elegant legs. "I think you missed your calling, Matt. You should have been a trial lawyer."

Matt raised his eyes and stared at her. "So you ruined the dinner?"

Smiling languidly, Pamela reached for another cigarette. Her every action was weighted with cynicism. "Yes."

"Why?" Matt's voice was filled with incomprehension.

But Pamela wasn't watching Matt. She had turned her ice-blue eyes on Casey, but the ice had melted. In their place was something like sorrow. "When I found out that you had asked Casey to come to the Cape, I tried to think of a way to keep her from coming. I wanted you for myself." She glanced back at Matt. "Or hadn't you realized?"

He shook his head and she went on. "Alonzo Davis had approached me to try to set up a meeting with you, but you had made it clear that you wouldn't meet with him. But he kept bugging me, so I thought it'd be perfect to use him to get rid of Casey. I told him that Casey was catering here during May and that you had great faith that her cooking would get Stefanos to sign with you. I convinced Davis that if he could woo her away, the deal between you and Stefanos would fall through."

Matt grinned ironically. "What's really funny is that I used that as an excuse to get Casey to come to the Cape with me, but it's just not true. Stefanos is picky, sure, but I'm a good enough businessman not to have to rely on a woman's cooking to clinch a deal." He sent an apologetic glance toward Casey, but she barely noticed it. She was too intent on trying to figure out what he had meant, about using it as an excuse to get her to come to the Cape with him. Why? For a month-long love affair, or because he cared for her?

"Anyway," Pamela continued, "I made sure Kevin got that picture so I'd have some hard evidence, but then it fell through. Casey refused the job with Davis and I forgot all about it until Anna mentioned that he was seen in Provincetown. I knew Casey was driving all over the Cape, so I thought of the idea of warning you about her and him. As it turned out, I got lucky. On the exact day I warned you here in the study, she ended up going to Provincetown."

Casey stared at Pamela, beginning to see how she had worked one against the other. While telling Matt that Casey was probably Alonzo Davis's lover, she was also telling Casey that Matt was getting tired of her and would never want to marry her. But why? How could she have developed such a loathing for Casey? Had she loved Matt so desperately? Sitting forward, Casey implored Pamela. *"Why, Pam? Why have you done all this? At times I've felt you actually hated me."* This was what she needed to know. This was the question she had wondered about from the very beginning. What had she ever done to make Pamela Tyrone dislike her so?

Pamela sighed and rubbed her eyes tiredly, then looked at Casey. "Where do you think I come from?"

Casey shrugged, not understanding the question. "What do you mean?"

"What town?"

"Wellesley, perhaps," Casey said, naming a wealthy suburb of Boston. "Someplace like that." It was obvious that Pam came from a well-off and cultured family. Why was she asking such a strange question?

Pam laughed softly. "I come from a little mill town near Fall River. My mother and father worked in the mills and thought I'd end up there too, but I surprised them. I got out and started making myself into a new person. I changed my name from Patricia Houlihan—I'm Irish, too, Casey—to Pamela Tyrone, got myself a scholarship to a secretarial school, and went to Boston. Last year I got the interview with Matt and decided I not only wanted to work for him, I wanted to marry him." She shrugged. "Why not? I'd accomplished everything else I'd set out to do."

Then the defiance left her face, leaving Pamela looking particularly vulnerable. Her lips began to tremble, but she took an enormous breath and regained control. "It was going so well, Casey. Matt and I were working well together, and I was even staying over at his house when we worked late. It was just a matter of time. Then I saw that article on you in the paper. I felt almost a kinship with you. You were Irish too, and had been poor, and you'd worked up from nothing, just like me. But I left the article on my desk and Matt picked it up."

Her eyes seemed to go blank as she looked into the past. "You should have seen his face, Casey. Absolutely absorbed. And he kept looking at your picture." She shook her head and Casey saw the tears glittering unshed in her eyes. "And he put that article down and said, 'Call her. She's exactly what I want.' And I knew right then that you were going to be the one who kept me from getting Matt Stoner. I think I hated you from that moment on. It's strange, isn't it, because I felt like I'd identified with you." She sighed and went on. "Anyway, I arranged for you to walk in on Matt and Crystal because I knew how he hates for people to walk in unannounced, but even *that* didn't work." She smiled ruefully. "I guess I should have given up then."

Pamela closed her eyes and bowed her head, then shrugged. "I don't know what happened in your life, Casey, but it sure mustn't have been like mine. I've had to grow a shell to protect myself, and I've gotten hard and cold. You're soft. You're warm." She laughed bitterly. "I guess men like warm women in bed with them at night."

Casey sat and stared at Pamela, feeling that same sense of compassion she had felt earlier. But what could she say? That she understood? That their childhoods must have been different? What small comfort was that? She made a motion toward Pamela, as if reaching out to her. "But your shell's broken now, Pam. You're not ever going to hide behind it again."

Pamela smiled a tough, brittle smile. "Says who? You know what I'm going to do, Casey Adams? I'm going to find a rich man and marry him and never have to worry about anything again as long as I live."

Casey nodded sadly. Yes, and she would become one of those rich, brittle women who were always wisecracking to hide their pain and disillusionment.

Pamela stood up and waved a hand lazily. "I'll pack and be on my way. If you could find it in your heart to give me a reference, Matt, I'd be grateful."

Matt nodded grimly, then Pamela turned and walked from the room. Once again, quiet descended. Casey stared at the floor, feeling an attack of nerves erupt in her stomach. Now what was going to happen? She had been vindicated about the dinner, but what about her and Matt? Nervous, afraid of what was coming, Casey got up and paced the room.

"I feel sorry for her," she said, trying to make some sort of innocuous conversation.

Matt said nothing, just followed her movement around the room with his gray, unrevealing eyes. Casey stopped, picked up a book, and leafed through it, not seeing a word on any page, then put it down again and went on, drifting about the room aimlessly, her nerves almost at fever pitch. Finally Matt spoke.

"Why *did* you take all those drives around the Cape, Casey, if not to meet another man?"

Casey rubbed her hands together, feeling cold. What could she tell him? That at first she had been enjoying the sights, but that later they became an escape from the tension in his elegant home? What should she do? Pretend to him or tell the truth? She bit at her lip and fretted. If she couldn't tell the man she loved the truth, then something was drastically wrong and there could be no future for them. She must take the risk. She must tell him about her fears. That was the only way she would ever find out how he felt, if he thought she could ever fit into his world.

"At first I was just relaxing, being a tourist," she said, smiling jauntily, but then her smile faltered and died.

"And then?" Matt prompted gently.

She heard the gentleness in his voice and found the courage to go on. "And then it became a kind of escape."

Matt frowned. "An escape? From what? There weren't any pressures here, were there? My God, Casey, you run a huge, successful business in Boston and don't need to escape."

Casey gnawed at her thumbnail, a practice she usually detested but one that her nerves made necessary right now. "It was a different kind of pressure here, Matt." She searched for words vainly, then opened her arms wide, gesturing around the room. "It's all this. This wealth. This—" She ended lamely, "Money."

Matt's forehead became furrowed with lines. "But you're used to this. You've catered the wealthiest people in Boston."

"But that's just it, Matt!" she said passionately. "I've *catered* them, not lived with them. Not been part of them. I've never sat at those tables I set, never ate the food I prepared. I was always in the kitchen somewhere, or behind my desk in a professional capacity. I was safe there. But when I came *here*..." She trailed off, unable to find the words to express her deeply hidden fears. She hugged herself and turned away, lest he see the tears that were threatening to escape her green eyes.

She heard a chair squeak and then footsteps behind her. Gentle hands took hold of her shoulders and turned her around. Matt's face was filled with love and understanding. Compassion radiated from his eyes. "And when you came here, what happened, Casey?" he asked gently.

Why was he looking at her like that? Did he pity her? Was he feeling sorry for the little girl from Southie who didn't belong? Or was it possible, could he... Her thoughts broke off. She had to answer him. It was the only way she would arrive at the truth. She swallowed with difficulty and went on. "When I came here," she said slowly, "I realized something I'd never faced before—that, that . . ." She trembled, afraid to say the words.

"That what, Casey?" he asked softly, his hands still gentle on her shoulders.

"Well, I guess that I felt a little scared of all this money, Matt. I'm from a different world from yours. I grew up in Southie and my whole life's been, well, *different.*"

"So you didn't *always* eat caviar for breakfast?" he teased gently.

An answering smile quivered on her lips. "No, not always. More like oatmeal or an occasional poached egg on toast."

"And not off of expensive English bone china?"

"No, we had chipped melamine dishes for everyday. For *good,* we had a set of dishes that my mother got from the grocery store. One dish for every three dollars of groceries you bought." Casey paused, wanting to get all her doubts out in the open. "There's something else, Matt."

"Oh?" he asked, his voice still reassuring. "What's that?"

"Well, you . . . you put me in the little cottage by myself instead of up here in the big house, and I thought, I was afraid . . ."

"You were afraid of what?"

"That . . . that you thought I wasn't good enough, or that maybe I wouldn't fit in."

Matt put a finger under her chin to try to raise her face to his, but she resisted. She couldn't look at him. She just couldn't. Without pressuring her, Matt spoke quietly.

"I gave you the little cottage so we could have some privacy, Casey. If I'd put you in a room near mine, and then gone to you every night and the other guests had seen me, it would have degraded you. You're a fine and beautiful woman, Casey, and I couldn't do that to you."

She bit at her lip, feeling hope burgeon within her. Yet still she kept her eyes down, afraid to look up at him.

Matt's voice was filled with gentleness. "Casey Adams," he said softly. "Will you please look at me?"

She hesitated, staring instead at the buttons that marched up his shirt. Then she lifted wary eyes to his. Sunlight seemed to burst into her soul. He was looking at her with such warmth, such gentleness, such love, that she felt filled with light, as if someone had lit a thousand candles in her soul.

"Do you mean to tell me, Casey Adams, that you're afraid you wouldn't fit into my 'world,' as you put it?"

She nodded, but felt hope growing stronger in her heart, surging up inside her like a great stream of white water.

Matt was shaking his head back and forth, as if in wonderment at her. "Casey, do you know I've been looking for a woman exactly like you since I've been old enough to look at girls? A woman who looks every inch a lady, but who's warm and loving and responsive. A woman who's a lady in the world and a little bit of a whore in bed."

Casey's eyes widened in shock. "A *whore?*" Her green eyes flashed with volcanic anger, but when she tried to pull away, Matt held her closer, laughing softly.

"All right, I'll change the word. A woman who's a little wanton in bed." He stood back and examined her face, saw she still wasn't happy, and changed it again. "Oh, all right. A woman who's a *woman*, damn it, not some dry stick who lies there and thinks of England!"

As quickly as it had come, her anger died, leaving her filled with warmth and love. "When I'm in bed with you, Matt Stoner," she said, her voice shaking slightly, "I'm sure as hell not thinking of England."

Laughing, Matt pulled her into his arms. "Ah, my beautiful Casey, I think it's time we had that serious talk, don't you?"

Trembling, she could only close her eyes and cling to his hard, muscled body. She nodded, afraid to trust her voice.

"Well then, Casey," Matt murmured softly, his breath fanning her hair at her brow. "I think we better think pretty seriously about getting married."

She stood in his embrace, her eyes closed, feeling the sweetness and beauty creeping into her heart, warming her entire body. For so long she had been alone and she had managed. She was a real woman, a capable woman, one who could and did take care of herself, but something had been missing these past five years. Something incredibly beautiful and necessary. And that had been love—the rich, uplifting, hallowed state where two human beings joined together as one, confronted the world as one, cared for each other, supported each other, gave succor and sustenance, one to the other.

Lifting glowing eyes to Matt, Casey smiled at him, her love shining for him to see. "Yes, Mr. Stoner," she said softly. "I think we'd better give an awful lot of thought to that."

Second Chance at Love

___ 05703-7 FLAMENCO NIGHTS #1 Susanna Collins
___ 05637-5 WINTER LOVE SONG #2 Meredith Kingston
___ 05624-3 THE CHADBOURNE LUCK #3 Lucia Curzon
___ 05777-0 OUT OF A DREAM #4 Jennifer Rose
___ 05878-5 GLITTER GIRL #5 Jocelyn Day
___ 05863-7 AN ARTFUL LADY #6 Sabina Clark
___ 05694-4 EMERALD BAY #7 Winter Ames
___ 05776-2 RAPTURE REGAINED #8 Serena Alexander
___ 05801-7 THE CAUTIOUS HEART #9 Philippa Heywood
___ 05907-2 ALOHA YESTERDAY #10 Meredith Kingston
___ 05638-3 MOONFIRE MELODY #11 Lily Bradford
___ 06132-8 MEETING WITH THE PAST #12 Caroline Halter
___ 05623-5 WINDS OF MORNING #13 Laurie Marath
___ 05704-5 HARD TO HANDLE #14 Susanna Collins
___ 06067-4 BELOVED PIRATE #15 Margie Michaels
___ 05978-1 PASSION'S FLIGHT #16 Marilyn Mathieu
___ 05847-5 HEART OF THE GLEN #17 Lily Bradford
___ 05977-3 BIRD OF PARADISE #18 Winter Ames
___ 05705-3 DESTINY'S SPELL #19 Susanna Collins
___ 06106-9 GENTLE TORMENT #20 Johanna Phillips
___ 06059-3 MAYAN ENCHANTMENT #21 Lila Ford
___ 06301-0 LED INTO SUNLIGHT #22 Claire Evans
___ 06131-X CRYSTAL FIRE #23 Valerie Nye
___ 06150-6 PASSION'S GAMES #24 Meredith Kingston
___ 06160-3 GIFT OF ORCHIDS #25 Patti Moore
___ 06108-5 SILKEN CARESSES #26 Samantha Carroll
___ 06318-5 SAPPHIRE ISLAND #27 Diane Crawford
___ 06335-5 APHRODITE'S LEGEND #28 Lynn Fairfax
___ 06336-3 TENDER TRIUMPH #29 Jasmine Craig
___ 06280-4 AMBER-EYED MAN #30 Johanna Phillips
___ 06249-9 SUMMER LACE #31 Jenny Nolan
___ 06305-3 HEARTTHROB #32 Margarett McKean
___ 05626-X AN ADVERSE ALLIANCE #33 Lucia Curzon
___ 06162-X LURED INTO DAWN #34 Catherine Mills

All of the above titles are $1.75 per copy

Available at your local bookstore or return this form to:

SECOND CHANCE AT LOVE
Book Mailing Service
P.O. Box 690, Rockville Cntr., NY 11570

Please enclose 75¢ for postage and handling for one book, 25¢ each
add'l. book ($1.50 max.). No cash, CODs or stamps. Total amount
enclosed: $ _____ in check or money order.

NAME _____

ADDRESS_____

CITY_____ STATE/ZIP_____

Allow six weeks for delivery   SK-41

All of the above titles are $1.75 per copy

Available at your local bookstore or return this form to:

SECOND CHANCE AT LOVE
Book Mailing Service
P.O. Box 690, Rockville Cntr., NY 11570

Please enclose 75¢ for postage and handling for one book, 25¢ each
add'l. book ($1.50 max.). No cash, CODs or stamps. Total amount
enclosed: $ _____ in check or money order.

NAME _____

ADDRESS _____

CITY _____ STATE/ZIP _____

Allow six weeks for delivery.   SK-41

WHAT READERS SAY ABOUT
SECOND CHANCE AT LOVE BOOKS

"Your books are the greatest!"
—*M. N., Carteret, New Jersey**

"I have been reading romance novels for quite some time, but the SECOND CHANCE AT LOVE books are the most enjoyable."
—*P. R., Vicksburg, Mississippi**

"I enjoy SECOND CHANCE [AT LOVE] more than any books that I have read and I do read a lot."
—*J. R., Gretna, Louisiana**

"For years I've had my subscription in to Harlequin. Currently there is a series called Circle of Love, but you have them all beat."
—*C. B., Chicago, Illinois**

"I really think your books are exceptional . . . I read Harlequin and Silhouette and although I still like them, I'll buy your books over theirs. SECOND CHANCE [AT LOVE] is more interesting and holds your attention and imagination with a better story line . . ."
—*J. W., Flagstaff, Arizona**

"I've read many romances, but yours take the 'cake'!"
—*D. H., Bloomsburg, Pennsylvania**

"Have waited ten years for *good* romance books. Now I have them."
—*M. P., Jacksonville, Florida**

*Names and addresses available upon request